# PLAIN CRAZY IN PARADISE

# PLAIN CRAZY IN PARADISE

**A Noir Western Love Song**

*Examinations of Paradise No. 3*

## John Holt

# ABSOLUTELY AMAZING eBOOKS

Published by Whiz Bang LLC, 926 Truman Avenue, Key West, Florida 33040, USA.

For information contact:
Publisher@AbsolutelyAmazingEbooks.com

ISBN-13: 978-1945772559 (Absolutely Amazing Ebooks)
ISBN-10: 1945772557

**For Ginny**

"So, sure enough we put up partridges and, watching them fly, I was thinking all the country in the world is the same country and all the hunters are the same people."

**- Ernest Hemingway from *Green Hills of Africa***

# PLAIN CRAZY IN PARADISE

# CHAPTER 1
### Slightly Mad

**JOHN WESLEY GILL WASN'T DOING ANYTHING** right now other than sitting on the worn-smooth pine wood steps that led down from the front porch to the grass and tan dirt that was flecked with quartz and flakes of mica. He liked to sit here for hours examining a naturally occurring prickly pear cactus garden prospering a slight rise near the house and a few feet from a bucket-sized hole in the ground that lead to a den that was home to a large, surly badger. The deep growl would emanate from the darkness every time John Wesley walked the perimeter of the cactus admiring the soft green of the plants and the softer reddish pink of the flowers in late spring. He'd only seen the animal a few times, usually skulking off in the silver-white light of a full moon. A strange animal full of secrets he thought. A lot like me, so the badger had become a part of his life in an ephemeral way. The land covered by the prickly pear seemed to grow in spurts every few years by 25 to 30 square feet. After scanning this piece of ground his gaze would drift off across the rolling hills and swales that were covered in tall grass, rich green now in late spring, off past the grazing Hereford cattle, some horses, and small bands of antelope. He saw beyond all of this, actually seeing the view from here without really looking, staring until the landscape transformed itself into a series of transparent planes that shone lightly with the greens, blues, whites, reds and yellows of the land - a section of sky vibrating, a piece of ridge lifting away, a jagged band of mountains floating to him, the shapes gliding among and through each other. His mind moved with

*1*

them until he was standing in the white, hot, dusty alkali of Willshaw Flats or along the brushy streamcourse of Willow Creek or on top of the crest of the windswept Hudson Bay Divide over on the Blackfeet Indian Reservation. Gill did all this while sitting on his steps. And that's about all he'd done for the past week. Hell, he really hadn't done much of anything in the past fifty-five years, except write some poems, catch a lot of fish, hunt when he needed to, and raise hell with mining survey stakes at hard rock operations around Montana.

Years ago a big time country star turned one of those poems of his into a hit that made him lots of money and he'd sold a few others and they made him a little money off and on, every now and then. He lived cheap. Liked to do so in fact, so he got by. He knew how to put words together so they meant something, sometimes many things that all wove together and became something larger and he knew how to put these words together so that they made a kind of lyrical sense, but fame had eluded him or, more properly, he'd intentionally eluded it by hiding out on his small spread located at the base of Middle Butte of the Sweet Grass Hills in the north central part of the state just a beer or two's drive south of the Alberta border.

His place had good water, electricity, a wood kitchen stove, fireplace, wrap-around porch and a damn fine trout pond lay just over the hill down in Mosquito Draw. The water was filled with fat rainbows that liked to leap for the sky and slap the water with their tails on the few evenings when a hard, hell-bent wind wasn't roaring down the west slope of his butte, the one he called Gold Butte not Middle like on the maps. 'The power of that mountain scares the hell out of me," he'd think. 'But it's like gold. Can't get enough of it.' The butte was a nexus for him. All that was the

West rolled away in every direction and was reached first by the dirt track that led from his home to a gravel road and then to a highway and from there to anyplace. Like a river these paths became a free-form drainage that spilled out away from Gold Butte. And the butte was a focal point of power, an isolated mountain that mirrored or perhaps dictated his moods and perceptions. One morning he'd risen in an angry frame of mind for no good reason and when he looked up at Gold Butte, a wicked, black swirling mass of clouds was boiling down on him along the west slope. The rest of the sky was as blue as possible. Not another cloud or wisp of fluffy moisture anywhere. The self-contained storm worked its way across the sage-covered bench above him, the weather hissing and spitting rain and sleet as it gathered itself into a ball of malevolence that crashed over John Wesley before dissipating its natural rage in a cluster of devil winds and rain over his trout pond. Then the mean cloud was gone, like it had never been around to begin with. And there were those fierce winds filled with heat that made him sweat on a cool day; or complete calm while nasty thunderstorms blasted the country to within a few miles of the butte, which stood strong and serene beneath a peaceful sun. From his perch above the surrounding country he could look for miles and miles far south towards Sun River Country, west into the Rockies, east way out across the prairie, north to the wandering coulees and bluffs that drifted to Canada.

Living here alone with his thoughts was his life. No responsibilities. No one in his vision to worry about. No women. Every time he grew close to one he grew scared of losing his privacy and most importantly, his autonomy. One day they would be there and the next long gone. He'd tell a friend that they just left saying little or nothing. He'd say "I guess to know me is not to love me," laugh a little, light a cigar and take a slug of Beam from an always-present bottle. He had sufficient money to live on, to buy food, pay his few bills, drink his whiskey and smoke his cigars – Cuban or occasionally Dominican or Nicaraguan or even Honduran. He knew a lot about cigars and had acquired more than 40 books on the subject.

His passion for writing poetry, or twisted free verse as he liked to say, was mostly gone, a trail of greedy agents, corrupt New York publishing companies, and, worst of all, the venal, parasitic clowns who played at being friends lay scattered in the dusty, morose wake of his past. This was why he never followed up on that recorded poem that made him a little bit famous. The exhausting drag of half-assed, pretentious readings and bookstores and universities scattered along the road, a predictable grind that was only partially ameliorated by the quick fix of manipulating a crowd, the hangers on, the vain and mostly pointless act of self promotion - he didn't need any of it back then, didn't want any part of it now.

"Yeah I can write hard-core when I want, but why bother," he'd say to a friend who might have stopped by around sunset to drink a little and smoke some cigars. "But why the hell bother. No one listens anymore and I take no pride or satisfaction in the business. Rap. Hip-hop. Hack pedants pretending at being modernist poets. One-dimensional, plastic crap masquerading as music sung by bimbos and morons. Lunatic jive. Fuck it. The land's all that matters now, or ever did when I think about it. Bastards cuttin' it up all over the place. An artsy-fartsy no account writer selling out the Yaak Valley over in the northwest corner of the state. Shitting in his own nest for a buck and a little notoriety. And now a Canadian mining company's got their greedy eyes on Gold Butte," and he'd wave a hand over his shoulder in a direction that carried from his chair on the front porch through the main room into the kitchen and out the back screen door on up the gradually steepening grass hill, and charcoal-colored scree slope that arched its way into the night to the top of the volcano shaped mountain that was one of three standing together here keeping a silent guard over the land that rose and fell like gigantic waves out on the high plains. "They want to blast it to pieces, pour cyanide all over the rock and for what? To make gaudy jewelry people can wear around their necks like a noose." He'd draw down deeply on his cigar and add, "The land's all I care about. Not most people. Sure as hell not me. The land. That's all. That's it." And he and the friend would drink more whiskey and puff on cigars as they watched the moon come up over the south flank of the butte.

A pack or two of coyotes would howl and whoop at the eternal sight and when one of the big, bright planets would show itself, the animals would raise a ruckus over this rhythmic appearance, too. And the men would drink some more and John Wesley Gill would be thinking to himself, "Only thing I'm proud of is my love of this land. How I've always cared about it. I'm not good with people and caused more bad than good with all the women I've known," and an uneasy feeling would rattle through his guts because he also knew one more thing. That he was supposed to do something about the "greedy sons-of-bitches" that were tearing the heart out of the West. The gold, the silver, uranium and coal mining, the logging that savaged the mountains, the developers feeding like starving pigs at the yupster money trough with their gated communities, shoddily built condos and water-sucking golf courses, the oil and gas industry, the ski industry "and on it fuckin' goes," he'd say.

The world was changing too fast for Gills' taste. The landscape was being bulldozed, re-contoured, bastardized into a nightmarish vision spawned by technological maniacs determined to destroy the natural world in their own twisted image. Cow towns like Miles City and Choteau are becoming neon lit, fast paced highway strip development joints. Fast food. Wal-Marts. Quick Lubes. Credit-card-driven convenience store gas stations. Late-night TV talk show hosts with their "little spreads out in Montana." Twenty-five years ago fly fishing was considered at best an esoteric pursuit practiced by hapless souls suffering from some sort of brain malfunction. Today the rivers are clogged with greedy, high-tech guides driving the clients ("Clients" John Wesley would say to himself like it was a dirty word) down the Yellowstone, Missouri, Blackfoot and the Bitterroot. 'The Bitterroot," he'd say out loud to himself. "What a sweet river, and those California CPAs and junk bond crooks killed her off. Gone. All the way gone.' The armada of drift boats and rafts was largely comprised of wealthy, over-equipped ahead-of-the-recreational curve sports who cared little or nothing for the rivers they were on, the land they flowed through or the trout, unless they were over twenty inches. And fifth-generation family ranches were rapidly becoming quaint, shadowy images of a romantic past. Billionaires were buying them up in bunches with their pocket change. Charles Schwab and his cookie-cutter Stock Farm hideousness with its covenants requiring either faux farmhouse layouts, 15,000-square-foot "cabins" or so-called mountain rustic designs along the foothills of the Sapphires and a real fancy Tom Fazio-designed golf course. 'Yeah, that's the Montana I know and love. You bet," Wesley would growl, again to himself and the wind. Things are changing in a hell of a hurry out West and to Gills' tired eyes, the change is hellish.

A month or two back another friend of his, a rare and most uncommon woman visitor who'd known him way back when, said "John Wesley, quite bitching and write your poems about this damn good country that you say you care so much about. Do something. Get a collection together. Then call every damn editor you've got from New York to LA, maybe even your old agent will talk to you, but just get it done. Do it. Stop complaining. Do it. Now. So what if it only sells a few copies. You've always said it's the writing of the ideas that counts, not the bucks. Get off your dead ass and write. Maybe then you won't drive off the good ones like Agua Bonita. Where would she flee to anyway?"

"Back home to some place on the side of the road up there in the boreal forest called Indian Cabins just south of the Northwest Territories in Alberta, no doubt never to be seen again. At least that's what the note said. She literally walked out with her backpack and must have hitched her way north. Never heard another word. Gone is gone. After they leave they're gone, that's all."

He looked at her and thought about this for a bit then raised his lean, six-two body from his chair and said to the woman visitor who he'd slept with on occasion and actually liked, "You've always been a constant in my life. A good friend and your ideas matter, but for now, leave me be. The less you have to do with me the better off you'll be. " He looked down on her, into her honest brown eyes and he showed her nothing but his need to be alone and, what she was able to see where others couldn't, his pain and anger about his life and all that had and hadn't happened. Then he walked down the grassy hill and over the slight rise to the pond to see the rainbows jump and arc in the orange-red glow of the sun as it dropped behind the

Rocky Mountain Front eighty miles away. He watched the trout leap and crash back through the quicksilver surface of the still water and he watched the dust her car raised on the two-track as she drove off towards the town of Shelby and some cheap motel room to kill off the night by herself before she headed back home to Council Bluffs. But since the visit he'd been unable to get her idea out of his head. The notion kept playing round and round, over and over like some long-gone cigarette jingle. "Write your poems. Call in every damn favor. Get it done."

He'd make lists of places he'd spend some time in and write poems about. Country like the Musselshell a little south of here, the Poplar River drainage over east, the Missouri Breaks, Grande Cache up Alberta way, the Blackstone Plateau in the Yukon, Arizona canyon country and maybe the Middle Fork of the Powder River Canyon down in Wyoming. Places like that. He'd always crumple the lists up and toss them in the fire, but every day or so he'd make another, and he started working with the words again. He'd worked up most of a poem about the imagined journey that was growing closer to real in his eyes like another one of his shining planes. He called it **Plain Crazy** and the words began …

> *out where it's empty*
> *wind talks*
> *rain is an uncommon friend*
> *there are some strange people*
> *blown away*
> *by the electric hum of nothing*
> *running small stores*
> *growing weeds in the dust*
> *real drunk …*
>
> *… we're all linked together*

*by the white light express*
*that ties all of us*
*in a twisted knot*
*mountains blast out of nowhere*
*screaming in the sky*

"That's it, damnit," he'd said one night, as he stared at too many stars up above him. "Screaming in the sky. That's it."

~ ~ ~

That demon idea of hers wouldn't let go and there was country he wanted to see again. He wanted to burn some miles on the road. Highways, dirt roads, two tracks, no tracks. Get in the Suburban and drive all night under a new moon moving across the purple darkness above, windows rolled down, cool air rushing in filled with the scents of sage, fresh-cut hay, road dust. He wanted to drive too fast dodging mule deer feeding in the ditches just barely visible at the edges of the headlight beams, the lights spooking owls from their perches on old fence posts. And he wanted to pull into old camps in the dark, throw a tarp and sleeping bag down on the ground, lie on his back and wait for the countless stars to knock him out. He'd think about nothing for as long as he could then he'd think about the freedom of having nothing to do and everywhere to go.

So Gill called in a favor from a friend who was an editor at a large publishing house, a guy who produced his three collections years ago. Gill's idea, or his version of her idea, about writing poems about the land and its plight and maybe going back on a reading tour, hooked his editor friend, who, in an excited voice, told him that when he finished this collection, he'd publish it and arrange a promotional swing around the country and up in Canada. He'd see about getting the thing marketed. "Nothing big, John Wesley. Maybe eight to ten thousand to start. I'll send a contract and advance ten K for the project. No one in the industry will touch you these days, especially after you cold-cocked that guy from Columbia at the Grammys after they honored the song based on your poem."

Gill laughed and said, "The whiskey made me do it and he was an asshole."

His friend also laughed, though a touch nervously, and agreed but added, "You can't do that shit, buddy and breaking into that studio and burning the masters to songs based on your poems. Nearly drove old Dwight nuts. Took him a year to record another tune. You and It's A Beautiful Day. You're all crazy. Destroy you're own work. Plain crazy. Shit ... well, shit. Maybe I can use that to market you. 'The old bastard's back. Good as ever and as big a pain in the ass as ever.' We'll see. The book's a done deal, man. I owe you," and the friend hung up wondering if Gill could write as well as he used to, which was damn good or if he might be even better. "Love to see you up on the stage again working those literary shits over, John Wesley. Broadcasting that energy with that voice. That'd be something," he said in the direction of the phone, but it didn't respond.

John Wesley thought back on the weeks he'd spent while this friend kicked both whiskey and codeine at his place some years back. The screaming, convulsions, crawling on the floor to the bathroom, hands shaking so bad Gill had to drop the Librium in the poor guy's mouth for him. The sweats. The paranoia. All of it. His friend was off the booze and drugs now for seven years and that was no easy trick in this stab-you-in-the-back business and world. 'He doesn't owe me for that. He's always been there,' he thought.

He serviced his '83 Suburban, put a new set of Cooper tires on the rig, updated its music system – the CD player was banged-up, battered, shot, and made plans to check out some places he'd been to many times before and some he'd never seen but had a feeling about. Like the memory of an old buddy, the Musselshell River around Two Dot came to mind and the next day he'd make the two-hundred-plus mile run down there. He thought of his lady friend, cursing her and laughing at the same time. She always did things like this to him. He'd be sitting alone minding his own business with no plans and no particular place to go. Happy in his stasis, cynicism and loneliness. Then she'd call out of the blue or appear as if by magic standing in front of him like this last time and she'd plant something in his head that she knew he couldn't resist. Like the notion for the poem that made him lots of money or buying this place with some of that cash. She never seemed to leave him alone and he could always hear her voice wandering around in the back of his mind.

"Damnit all to hell. She knows how to get to me and she knows I can't let a good idea go. Damn her, wherever she is now. Death of me, that one," and he drew deeply on a Partagas Lusitania, took a long hit of Jim Beam and laughed again. "She's the only one I'd try like hell never to hurt."

Jupiter jumped up over the horizon and two packs of coyotes began chattering and yipping among themselves, the soaring, high-pitched canine talk slicing through the cool night air, soaring and echoing from ridge to bluff to hill to ridge. The animals' voices are visible to him gliding through the air. The sound looked like fluctuating, silver-white sine waves that connect the land with pure wild fluorescence. John Wesley can hear their trickster calls long after the sound has died on the wind. He leans back in his chair, re-lights his cigar and works on the whiskey.

~ ~ ~

He loves the Musselshell River for its quiet power and beauty, and for its brown trout. Always has. The trout are sunk down in the water hiding under the deep undercut banks where the small river twists and curves beneath tall cottonwoods that stand above the grassy banks of willow and alder. There are lots of browns here and they leap when he hooks them, their bloody-copper spots, bronze backs and yellow sides glisten in the light. The numbers and sizes of trout in a stream tell Gill about the health or sickness of a given piece of water and this translates to an overall picture of the drainage. Plenty of fish in a variety of age classes swimming in cool, clean water said to him 'Things are still okay here.' The valley is largely unchanged in the thirty years he's been fishing the river. Vast ranches full of cattle grazing on high-protein native grasses, thick pine forests cloaking the mountain slopes with few signs of clearcutting, the exposed cliffs and faces of the Crazies - the igneous intrusions, magma blisters and lava dikes, all of those surreal yet ordered geologic shapes that are only lightly softened by the erosive passing of hundreds of thousands of years. The river's valley is surrounded by these mountains and the Castles and the Little Belts. Really nothing much has changed around here. About the same number of people and cows and Sandhill cranes and deer by the thousands and the browns. And the highway that winds through the valley was a touch smoother and wider than the first time he staggered in here one August night in 1970 driving an old, banged-up Chevy pickup. He liked the Musselshell from that first taste, the peaceful buzz of the land, the bunches of deer that grazed nearly invisible in the tall grass and, of course, the voracious browns.

Gill likes to fish a stretch of the river a few miles from the out-of-the-way town of Martinsdale that is little more than a bar, gas station, bed and breakfast, and farm supply operation. The raised grade of the long-abandoned Milwaukee road, rails long since hauled away for salvage, runs east-west on the north edge of town. A large, wind-blasted reservoir serves as home for big rainbows on the south side. The northern end of the Crazies loom in the distance. At this time of the year the fields that sweep up to those mountains' base are emerald green and hold lots of cranes that clack and squawk in pterodactyl fashion. He's often surprised the huge, light grey birds as he works his way upriver casting large woolly buggers tight to the banks. The cranes' heads and elongated beaks perched atop long, graceful necks will stoop and peer at him, then in a racket of beating wings and loud croaks the Sandhills lift slowly into the air before quickly gaining speed and whooshing off out of site riding the wind. Gill follows their flight as the ancient birds became diminishing silhouettes against the blue-green forested backdrop of the mountains and the dark blue sky. On sunny days such as this warm June one, puffy cumulous clouds slide across the peaks of the Crazies, their billowing white surfaces turning countless shades of yellow, orange and pink as the sun begins to set. He loves fly fishing, less and less for the catching, and more as the seasons passed for days standing hip deep in rivers such as this one that flow to its own laid back tune through country such as this. He likes feeling a part of the system, connected with the river and all that goes with the process.

Gill is about a mile downstream from his camp, a place he's spent more nights than he can remember standing around small fires and drinking whiskey in the dark while meteors fizzle above him and the broad, white band of the Milky Way glows north to south, horizon to horizon. The only sounds are the gentle bubbling of the Musselshell as it wanders over its rocky bed or drifts along smooth flats, the talk of nighthawks booming as they swoop and dive after mayflies, caddis and mosquitoes, the sporadic bellowing of cattle in distant fields, the rustling of the grass and the barking of coyotes. Great Horned Owls live along the riparian corridor and they hoot their hearty, high calls throughout the night.

The colors of sunset are now turned to the velvet purples and growing blacks of evening. The edge of the western horizon hums silver-turquoise with the last of the day's light. Gill casts one last time tight against a bank where the water curls in above a tangle of willow roots. He lets the streamer settle as the current carries it beneath the bank then starts stripping in line and immediately, just as the Bugger clears the bank and comes out to open water, a huge brown, jaws wide open to the extent they he can see the whiteness of the trout's mouth even in the growing darkness, slams down on the fly with an audible snap and a tremendous whooshing and splashing from its thick form, the spray sparkling like subtle diamonds in the light of a rising, nearly-full moon. The fish crashes and sails up and down the river, smacking its tail on the surface and running in tight circles along the bottom, the line vibrating as the brown thrashes its head from side to side, Gill's delicate graphite rod bends in a U and pulses with the energy of the mad trout. Eventually the fish tires. He brings it to him in the shallow water at the tail of a riffle. The water burbles over the cobble as Gill admires the brown. Twenty-some inches, several pounds and those classic brown trout colors that radiate softly in the night. He unhooks the trout and holds it by the tail in the water, letting the oxygen-rich flow below the riffle revive the fish, that within seconds surges free of his hand and shoots to the shelter of the far bank with a quick flick of its tail. Gill follows the imagined course of the brown, smiles, shakes his head and says "Damn," and he knows she's right and is out in front of him on this idea. "The Musselshell. I can work with that." He walks out of the water to begin the hike back to camp through the forest of cottonwoods and thick brush, the embryonic form of a melody starting to run around in his head

The moon is high enough now to cast bright shadows ahead of him as he pushes through the undergrowth that crowds a well-used deer trail. His camp is west, upstream about twenty minutes worth of walking and he knows the way by heart. He pauses and lights a cigar with a stick match struck against the rough surface of a dead-fall, puffs on it several times blowing thick clouds of strong smoke towards the sky. Gill takes a deep breath of air, tasting the fertile nature of the river riding on the breeze - the fecund, sensual scent of the water, the lushness of the new leaves, the subtly mixed perfume of the wildflowers. He hears nighthawks cutting through the small open spaces in the trees, an owl hoot, a group of geese honking overhead as they return from a protracted feeding binge in some fields over the ridge, a coyote holds forth at the moon, and the leaves rustle gently as a warm night breeze moved down the valley. 'Paradise,' he thinks. Then he hears something else.

Well downstream the moaning, baying racket of a pack of hounds disrupts the night, the dogs barking crazily as they pursues their query. The canine cacophony closes in on him rapidly.

"Damn coon hounds move through this stuff a hell of a lot better than I do," he says to himself, and now they sound like they are within a few hundred yards of him and coming on fast. Then the report of high caliber rifles tears through the darkness, the bullets whamming into tree trunks above his head, pieces of scaly bark raining down on him. Gill yells "Fuck," and begins to run like he hasn't run in decades, crashing through the brush, scratching his arms on wild rose and raspberry thorns and ripping his shirt. He stumbles in a beaver hole as he nears the river and the grassy meadow by his camp. Falling, he slashes his hand on the sharp point of a small willow gnawed to a spear point by one of the beavers. "Shit," he yells and keeps running until he reaches the Suburban. Gill is soaked in sweat, covered in a mixture of his own blood, leaves, grass and mud. There's too much adrenaline zipping through his veins for him to feel any pain, only a mixture of anger and fear.

"Damn coon hunters. Nearly blew my head off," he mutters as he pours some whiskey in a blue enamel cup. He drains the booze off in one slash and pours some more. His hands are still shaking as he works on lighting his old Coleman white gas lantern. The mantel catches in a minor explosion of light and sound. He adjusts the flow of gas, sets the thing on his small camp table and sits down in a folding lawn chair he'd brought along. "Damn wimp," he says to himself and remembers the not too long ago days when camping was nothing more then pulling into a place like this, tugging on his waxed-cotton coat, and lying down on the ground until the sun woke him. If it happened to rain, he rolled under the truck and had a couple of scars on his forehead from banging against the old Chevy's differential to prove it. He sips at the whiskey and puffs on a fresh cigar, calmer now. From the sounds of things, the hunters and dogs are about a quarter-mile away. He hears voices and the sound of a truck tailgate and doors slamming.

"Must have parked it behind that bunch of trees back there," he offers to no one in particular and splashes a touch more bourbon in the cup, then builds a small fire of sticks and twigs in an old firepot he'd laid out the first time here.

He watches the headlights of the truck bob up and down, the yellowish light playing off the leaves and grass as the hunters and their dogs bounce along the rutted two-track. The truck pulls to a halt next to him. Three men in their twenties are crowded into the cab. The sound of the coon dogs' heavy breathing comes in rapid huffs from the wire and plastic kennels in the back.

The one driving, a blond fellow with a crewcut and wearing a white T-shirt with a pack of Marlboros rolled up in one sleeve, says, "We didn't know anyone was down here. Been huntin' coons and sure don't want anyone shooting the dogs by accident. They don't come cheap."

"Shit. You damn near shot me and I damn near shot back," Gill says. "Might want to consider that fact next time you're out here tearing hell out of the night."

The driver gives him a hard look and says, "We can take care of ourselves.

Gill laughs.

"I think it's only fair to warn you that you are in the presence of a man with a lighted lantern and he knows how to use it." He blows a stream of cigar smoke into the cab and works on his whiskey some.

The three look at him like he's crazy. He knows he's nuts. Muddy, sweat-soaked shirt. Blood and leaves plastered to his face and scattered all through his matted, thick greying hair. A twig is wedged behind one ear like a number two pencil. Glowing, hissing lantern in one hand. Tin cup in the other. Cigar jammed in the corner of his mouth. 'Famous poet savages local coon hunters' thinks Gill and a twisted grin dances across his unshaven face.

More silence, then the driver laughs with an edge of hysteria. "Well, we got to be off. Good night to you," and the pickup moves down the road.

Gill watches the headlights play over the land as the truck lurches and bounces up to the highway.

"I've always believed killing to be easy," he thinks. "Maybe I should have done those clowns for the hell of it." His eyes follow where the coon hunters' truck must have gone and he spits on the dirt. "Should have done it."

He turns to his pen and notebook, after building another drink and the words move in step with his internal rhythms like they always do when he's on his game. In a little more than an hour he finishes **Plain Crazy**. He tosses some wood on the fire, works on a fresh drink, smiles a touch and recites his poem all the way through just because he likes what he's created and he wants to hear all of it again, and he comes to the final bit ...

> *... large creatures wander fearless*
> *disrupting the current*
> *with their curious buzz*
> *snow and ice sweep down*
> *cattle freeze*
> *minds vanish*
> *the beating moves in constant time*
> *and is hard to disguise*
> *but the trick to this*
> *is to skip off to oblivion*
> *and enjoy the view ...*
>
> *... we're linked together*
> *by the white light express*
> *that ties all of us*
> *in a twisted knot*

*mountains blast out of nowhere*
*screaming in the sky ...*

... As his voice fades and melds with the land around him John Wesley knows that he still has his gift, and more importantly he now understands that she's right, that her vision is clear, pure. He has miniature tales to write, in his own wandering, lyrical way and in his own time, which is right now.

# CHAPTER 2

## No Reservation Required

**HE LIVED ONLY AN HOUR** or so east of this country, but for some reason, hell, for many reasons, he'd avoided coming onto the Blackfeet Reservation for more than a dozen years. Browning, the main town on the Rez, depressed him to no end. Wind-blown, pounded by relentless gales that swept down from the summits of the nearby mountains, garbage, plastic bags, beer cans swirling every place, abject poverty, crumbling government housing – urban visited upon the high plains. The main motel's sign blown apart, blown down. Attempts at attracting tourists like the modern and well-done museum that draws a few visitors who are usually terrified by the surroundings and leave before spending money on anything but gas and maybe some dried-up fried chicken at the Exxon plaza on the east side of town next to Highway 2 that heads out along the prairie and thankfully out of the place funneling the tourists to places like Havre, Glasgow and way out there Wolf Point. Hi-Line communities of relative familiarity to these Anglo foreigners. You know, the familiar stuff – Burger King, McDonald's, MiniMart, 7-Eleven, Golden Spike Bar, TireRama, the Colonel, Best Western, Super 8, Stockman's Bar, Alibi Lounge – all the usual nightmare familiar stuff that cons the traveler into thinking he's having a good time in a new-found piece of country.

'Horrible,' he always thinks both about Browning and the tourist road in general. When Gill stops at Ick's Place on a side street called North Piegan just off the main drag located conveniently just a cold one away from the Drug Rehab center, and passes his money through the barred window to pay for his whiskey or vodka or whatever, he knows he's being watched with a feeling like the most vulnerable of prey licking through his veins. He senses the cold stares that feel like icy bugs crawling up his neck and the back of his head. By the time he's returned to his rig parked twenty feet away on a street filled with empty, busted booze bottles, candy wrappers, Marlboro cigarette packs and dog shit, a half-dozen drunk, drugged-out, hungover Indians are waiting for him and a handout. They swirl around him like wraiths. Men, boys already dead, a couple of teenage girls skinny and vacant-eyed from booze, drugs, hooking and little food, from sleeping in dumpsters pushed up against walls in some dirty alley resembling large rusting green coffins. They circle and shuffle like starved, thirsty, dissipated wolves that will kill for what they want if they can. They will do this if Gil leaves the smallest of openings in his retreat to the vehicle. Money, booze, clothes, his cigars. Anything that is free, that they don't have to labor for is fair game. Hunting season on the Rez is always open.

"Hey man, how 'bout some money so we can drink, too," they say with an obvious tone of threat. "Give us a drink of your whiskey, man, okay, huh?"

Gill sights in on all of them with a cold stare and says "No," walks over to the driver's side and heads off out of town with a sense of relief that feels like the first rushes of those Percodan pain killers he sometimes takes for his bum knee, the one he injured many years ago playing football in high school and really tore up jumping out of the way of a surly moose in the thick brush along the upper Stillwater River, a class act stream ripping down from the Whitefish Mountains in the northwest corner of Montana a couple of decades back. After about fifteen windy highway miles that bring the mountains of The Front into massive relief, filling his windshield with their snow-covered granite peaks and dense forested lower slopes, he turns down along a dirt road that edges the Rockies, a road that breaks off into lesser tracks that move far into the foothills, through canyons that guard creeks running out of the high country. Streams that hold native westslope cutthroat trout and bull trout. He takes a few hits on the booze, shaking his head and muttering, "God, what a place. I feel sorry for those poor bastards," but he never gives them money. Never once. He can't see his way around this even though he knows that if he were in their dire straits he'd be begging and threatening the people, also. He's crawled down that road, selling books, tossing furniture for change, begging from friends and relatives. The good life that seems to be well behind him now. He hopes so, anyway. He kicks his mind away from these too honest thoughts and grim images. The land up this way is spectacular, wild, extreme. Tall pines, ragged cliffs, turquoise water, a few deer – the lucky ones who haven't been poached by tribal members at all times of the year. No seasons. No Limits. Just rifled slaughter by the Blackfeet trying to feed themselves. Already words are running around his head and a name for the poem - **dancing nowhere** – flashes in his head like the liquor store neon he recently fled.

He's already decided, already knows that none of the poems will make even the vaguest attempts at conforming to anyone or anything literary. They'll drift and glide through their individual stories like mildly structured tales spun around late-night campfires. He'll do this his way. He doesn't need a contract, another book or the money, but he won't refuse any of this, either. He's doing whatever this is right now for himself or for land he cares about, really loves.

"Art for art's sake," he says around sips of liquor.

"What a fucking joke. Maybe the words will be for my sake. Shit," and he takes another hit, the whiskey burning his throat a little bit and glowing justly warm in his gut. He pulls over along the side of the road in the muddy, wet blue grama grass, already a couple of feet bright-green-stemmed tall. And he writes the words down quickly with a cheap pen in a small notebook that he keeps next to him in the Suburban.

> *the great American pastime*
> *crashing head on*
> *where the front is obvious*
> *not running down buffalo*
> *not looking for images in ice water*
> *or wandering*
> *after scapegoat seasons*
>
> *a lot of green thunderbirds*
> *discarded and smashed*
> *along dusty roadsides*
> *dead men gasping*
> *with whitewashed education*
> *draining from torn ears*
> *could not bank on truth*
> *reservations were not honored*
> *around chinookville ...*

He reaches down and grabs a Pabst from the small cooler on the floor, pops the sucker, foaming, he drinks most of it with not a thought to the madness, the illegality of driving and drinking, Montana's accepted pastime. He drifts back to the last time he was up this way driving through this insane, bizarre, wild country.

'Spring fishing on the Blackfeet Rez is:

The only truth is wind. Cold. Chinook warm. Strong. Blustery. Often from the north. Always.

The fish are big. The fish are small. Not around.

Surfing gale-generated waves. Hard to catch. Easy to catch. Schooled up by the hundreds, thousands. Rainbows. Cutts. Hybrid variations. Then gone again. Nowhere to be seen.

The weather always wins. The landscape is staggering. Surreal. Lonesome. It will snow. It will Rain. The sun will blast down. Browning is depressing. East Glacier is a tourist ghost town even in July. Freight trains rumble over Marias Pass. Tiny nymphs work as well as large streamers.

After twenty years doing this early-season stuff I've learned that I know next to nothing about the angling, the country or *The People* that live here,' is what Gill's thinking and the course of his memories and reasoning is flashing fast now. 'I've always been an outsider despite childish pretensions otherwise, thinking I was a friend while being pimped for PR. That's how it goes. No big deal. The return my way has been fair. Money for stories or book chapters. Wild country. Huge fish. A touch of freedom. Unexplained visuals that spin around bluffs or race along ridges. Blue-light-glows arcing from the tops of buttes. Extraordinary howlings. Unusual footprints. Rumors of women gone missing, maybe murdered. The usual suspects.

I've caught trout over ten pounds a few times on waters called Mission, Duck, Goose, Kipp, Twin. Brook. Cutthroat. Rainbow. Brown. Hybrid. A rogue Bull. That's what he's thinking right now.

But I don't know anything up this alien way. Alien to my soft, white mind. Rhythms, techniques, dictions all beyond me.

Summer. Autumn. A bit calmer, vaguely familiar, feeling safer.

Spring means hardball. All the juice turned loose after a dark winter's frozen dormancy. Moving along muddy two-tracks next to Cut Bank Creek. Opening, closing rusting barbed wire gates. Spending a ghostly night in an abandoned radar base barracks eating canned beef stew. Drinking whiskey. Smoking a lot of Camel straights. Listening to my fear creaking through twisted, corroded beams and rotted window frames. Even the pigeons don't spend the night in this place. Coyotes howl near daybreak. Saying "Thank god" to the sunrise and looking left across the border into Alberta before catching a couple of big fish in a nearby creek. Whitetails running at my motion. Crop duster landing his beater biplane just over my head on a red dust road in front of me. Eagles soaring with more grace higher up the sky. Looking for rabbits, mice, voles.

Vicious winds tear down from the Front blowing everything ahead of their course. Russian thistle, clumps of sage brush, license plates, cigarette packs, beer cans, crop land, ball caps, large rips of plastic that used to masquerade as storm windows, all of this sucked along in a swirling wake of confused detritus.

The Blackfeet.

Yeah I know them. Quite well. You bet. Not at all. Never will. How could I?

Browning. Heart Butte. Blackfoot. Government housing. Abject poverty. A sense of humor that mocks me with no hope of entrance. Long-time tribal acquaintances seeing me as a means to an end. In the schools, on the streets, riding in cars - too much booze, too many drugs, just like everywhere, but way different on the Rez – poison taken to a bad land nomadic death trip. High-plains wanderers fenced in by the inevitability of modern change. Happens to all of us, but true murder for these people.

And even with all these imagined memories and images rattling around in my head, I've always come back here in the spring. Ice-out April. Paradise May. Wet June. Mountains running madly. Green grasses waving ocean visions. Wildflowers exploding. Rafts of cloud racing the sky.

Magnificent in its isolation despite its desolation.

And the fish. The times of hundreds of rainbows cruising at my feet. Enormous, dark silhouettes of twenty pounds. Mouths whitely agape in sexual excitement or maybe eating nymphs. Crimsons. Purples, Silvers. Fluorescent. Life lit up like a natural Vegas strip. Trout obsessed with false spawn. An illusion of procreation that can't be met in closed systems. Enormous rainbows that blast off and blow up a five-weight. Or dog a wind-cheating eight down deep until the game is up and the sullen fish is pulled defeated to shore. Only to be released. To pretend to breed some more. Metaphor for nothing.

I haven't been up to here in years. I want to give this place one more shot to see if good memories, high times from my Flathead Valley days remained. Does any of the crazed, somewhat demoralize magic remain or have I hammered through too many years and too many arcane mistakes to see anything up this way?

Is any of the illusion left?

Rolling magically upwards with my foot off the accelerator on a stretch of road my friends and I named "Zero Gravity Hill" years ago. Illusion in country driven by tilted horizon. I marvel at a ridge of cloud that stretches far into Canada and well to the south of Augusta behind me. The wall of moisture spins back on itself as it is torn between the updraft of The Front and a desire to roll on eastward across the high plains towards the Dakotas. I watch all this while keeping an eye on the highway largely empty of traffic today except for a random semi or pickup. I turn left on a lesser paved road, then right on another. Within a few miles I cut left on a dirt road that winds up into the foothills and mountains. A beautiful, familiar and some-times-fished stream sparkles alongside the serpentine, now rutted road as I drift through aspen only beginning to leaf out and through dense stands of old pine that are intense green with a new year's exuberance. The creek is flowing at a perfect level, its flow not yet marred by the riotous gushings of snowmelt and heavy spring rains. Caddis rise off the surface in the warming air. Clumsy, whirring flight unlike the delicate liftings of mayflies or the workmanlike efforts of stoneflies. A few rise forms mark the surface of long deep glides. This is one of the prettiest streams I've ever fished. Eagles, grizzly, elk, deer, moose, badger, marten, mountain chickadees, swallowtail butterflies later, and a few trout, mostly around a foot long, live in this drainage that seems to be little changed over the past fifty years. I always catch westslope cutthroat trout here on elk hairs and Royal Wulffs and Humpies with a light four-weight and a slight tippet. Maybe a Hare's ear nymph down below. The biggest was taken a half-dozen years back. Sixteen inches and a leaper. A cutthroat rarity. If the fish only ran to four inches I'd still hold this water, this undeveloped valley and canyon, close. A perfect place or nearly so and that's enough these days.

He drops down what's left of a rocky track and park out of sight beneath a thick copse of aspen. Pull on hip waders. Assemble a rod with a #16 Wulff at the tip. At the edge of the stream he stands and watches as a bunch of trout rise to caddis that are close to the size of the bug on his line. The trout work steadily in splashing, carefree takes that is this species' trademark. The hell with death. There's food about. Line is stripped off the reel. A quick cast below the fish to measure distance and then a quartering shot above the cuts holding lowest in the chain. A nice drift on the inside edge of the current seam and a take. A quick struggle and a ten-inch westslope cutthroat trout –

bright, black spotted, orange-red slashes below the jaw. Released it shoots for cover below its kind thirty feet away. Another cast. Another trout. Thirteen inches. Maybe. Same coloring. Nice. Working upstream to runs, glides, deep pools. Always fish. As good or better than remembered. In shallow riffles he shifts to the nymph and take cutthroat running about fourteen inches that are nosing the small gravels dredging caddis pupae.

In a few hours he looks up from the dancing water and sees that he's well above the canyon that marks the entrance into the mountains. Through the narrow view upstream snow-covered peaks glisten as snow begins to melt in the afternoon warmth. The sky is blue shading to silver-white in the hot light. A pair of red-tails works a ridge on my right. Sharp cries slice the stillness and mix with the talking water. Bending down on his knees, he drops his mouth to the surface and drinks the water that tastes of snow, gravel and tannin. The walk back takes awhile but seems like nothing. Tossing the gear in the back of the Suburban, he opens the cooler, grabs a beer, lights a cigar and enjoys what's left of the light. He'll find a motel room – TV, lousy pizza, neon, slamming car doors, whiskey, little sleep – in the dark, In Cut Bank. Later.

This day's been good. Tomorrow. Who knows? Maybe a lake or two. Possibly another stream like this one. The Rez has more than one. A couple more days alone. Ideal after a bad trip earlier this month, one riddled with commercialism and too much booze, melancholy. All this will be pleasant, peaceful, but honestly now after a couple of decades of consciously lying to himself, despite the fantastic country and the fish and all of this, the Rez is largely a sad experience. That's Gil's problem, but a real one. Poverty. Hopelessness. Future oil and gas development.

Guiding hucksterism.

As a late friend used to say "It's all going or gone." Feels that way here. Hopefully I'm wrong. The gut says I'm not. But then ...

Yeah it's weird and sad up here, John Wesley thinks. And I'll always feel like a stranger, but the land is beyond believing and the fishing can be great, so in a decade, give or take, when I'm well into my sixties, I'll more than likely wander back here in the spring.'

And his thoughts kick back to the words of this new verbal child. This one writes itself like the last number, like they all do when he's on the move this way.

> *... sliding along*
> *on fusel oil*
> *and ancient dreams*
> *kicked aside*
> *by forgotten collisions*
> *with rotted pickups*
> *the breeze drinks it all*
> *bone dry ...*

He pulls over at a wide spot in the road beneath an old, spread-out Ponderosa. The creek he plans to fish is running away about thirty feet below, bending its back in a large bow against an outcropping of green-grey Appekunny mudstone streaked with pink-white quartz that shows golden sparkles of iron pyrite – fools gold. Deep orange and faded green lichens coat the wall in patches. Above from a narrow ledge small pines hold tight in a thick carpet of vibrant emerald moss that seems to radiate the subtlest of lights. Water drips down from here marking the rock nearly black. As Gil rigs up his light four-weight rod he notices several large trout working along the base of the ledge. Fifteen, eighteen and one that looks to be twenty inches. All of them feeding on tan caddis that are whirring like confused helicopters above the stream's surface. The sun breaks out and highlights the water on a regular basis as it plays an intermittent disappearing act behind cumulous clouds that shuffle off rapidly towards the vastness of the eastern high plains. The wind down in the canyon is moderate and cool as it moans softly through pine needles and aspen leaves. Several whitetail look down at him from the trees above the ledge, ears and tails flicking sporadically. Dark eyes glistening in the muted light.

He slides down the loose soil and rock, cautiously approaches the stream balancing from foot to foot on the rocky bank. He works out line and begins to false cast until he can cover the distance to the first fish, about forty feet. He shoots the Elk Hair caddis attached to the slender tippet well above the first feeding cutthroat bouncing the fly off the granite wall and into the water. The pattern glides down to the trout that rises easily and takes Gil's offering. He sets the hook and the fish struggles for cover along the streambed before running downstream then around in circles before he brings the fish to the shallows. Sixteen inches, firm, black spotted its entire length with silver and slight yellow shadings and large orange slashes along its lower jaw. Wild, native perfection. He twists the hook free of the trout's jaw and gently revives it in the weak current. Soon the cutthroat quivers, flicks its tail and shoots across the current. Out of sight. Gone. Vanished.

He works his way upstream moving along the cobbled bank beneath the Ponderosa and small stands of aspen. He catches four more, from the deep glide on the increasingly ragged caddis pattern. Each fish is slightly larger than the one before. The last is the twenty inches he estimated from above and colored a deep golden yellow along its flanks fading to a cream white along its belly. The echoes of the fish's splashing are turned to pure crystal by their contact with the rock walls. Gil turns this one loose and retreats to a large rock above the stream, the sound like wine glasses breaking far back inside a large ice cave. He lights another one of his Honduran maduro cigars, a Rothschild that fits in one of his pockets along with several others like they were designed for the shirt. He draws down deep several times, exhaling the smoke and watching it disperse on the breeze. He pulls a small flask from his shirt pocket. He never wears a vest, stuffing what he needs in various pockets. He only wears waders when it's truly cold out or he's high up in the mountains where the water feels like liquid ice. He takes a hit on the bourbon. Puffs the cigar some more and looks upstream.

A Blackfeet is standing there staring at him. Dark, way past walnut color, skin. Long black hair in braids tied with red strips of cloth. Plaid shirt. Faded jeans. Hiking boots. They lock onto each other. Blue eyes connected to black. No thoughts just a transference of the human buzz. The warrior, the word that comes to Gil's mind, his hard looking, muscular like a deep-brown variation of the granite across the way. They hold each other's gaze for a long time, then the Blackfeet breaks off and looks up above him at a towering cliff. Gil follows the gaze and sees petroglyphs halfway down, maybe two-hundred, three-hundred feet from the top. The drawings are faded brown-red like blood. Elk. Grizzly. Fires. Men dancing. Bison. Teepees. And one in the center of an individual with an aura of arrows radiating from his head towards the other drawings. He can see them all clearly even though they are far above him.

Hundreds of years old, he thinks. Elk fat, powdered rock and maybe a little slaughtered Kootenai Indian blood for richness of texture and color saturation, and he laughs a little to himself before turning to look back upstream. The warrior is gone like he was never there in the first place. Gil knows about these ones. Tribal members who are secretive, elusive, virtually invisible, moving like smoke or mist through the land, hiding out in the rough country of the canyons, forests and bluffs of The Front. A secret Blackfeet society operating outside the law, often wanted by the white man's legal agencies. Gil's heard of plans they've made for attacking the white tourists in the sellout town of East Glacier next to the National Park, and how they have thought out the dynamiting of Hungry Horse Dam forty air miles west across the Bob Marshall Wilderness on the South Fork of the Flathead River, and maybe Gibson Dam holding back the Sun on this side of the mountains and even a raid on Choteau and the so-called ranches of a self-important TV talk show host, some hack movie stars and a junk bond scam artist or two. And he's heard more along these lines and always hopes, fantasizes, that "the crazy bastards do it' and don't just trip along dreaming the plans away high on datura or mescaline or psilocybin. A little deadly mayhem would shake things up in the once wild west he thinks. A little death and destruction would do some good out here. Maybe they'll pull one or all of these plans off. That would be something to witness, he thinks.

Gil scans the drainage far upstream through trees and rock walls, maybe catching a glimpse of a shadowy shape ghosting around a bend, but doesn't really see a firm form of the Indian anywhere. Probably all of it was his overactive imagination or just some displaced hallucination. No matter. It was an entertaining interlude at the very least.

"Gone like a damn spook," he mutters standing up

and working a kink out of his lower back with a long stretching of his arms to the sky. Then he heads back to the truck, writes the end of **dancing nowhere** down in the notebook to free his head for more silliness, and drives east off the Rez to a cheap motel in Cutbank ...

> *... and even with all this*
> *withered death*
> *life thrives*
> *not too deep*
> *with room to hide*
> *in all the motion*
> *clear rises to the top*
> *trout scurry for cover*
> *noticeably in spring*
> *an out of control time*
> *caddis breaking loose*
> *floating in warm air*
> *slightly stirred*
> *from flow below*
> *logging trucks growl*
> *gunshots echo*
> *to little effect*
> *crystal now*
> *invisible*
> *cold*
> *when snow comes*
> *order compacts*
> *under the ice*
> *silence and dark dormant*
> *waiting to move again like a patient serial killer*

# CHAPTER 3

## Somewhat Confused

*"The sun was just setting when we crossed the final ridge and came in sight of as singular a bit of country as I have ever seen. Over an irregular tract of gently rolling sandy hills, perhaps about three-quarters of a mile square, were scattered several hundred detached and isolated buttes or cliffs of sandstone ... Some of them rose as sharp peaks or ridges, or as connected chains, but much the greater number had flat tops like little table-lands. The sides were perfectly perpendicular, and were cut and channeled by the weather into the most extraordinary forms: caves, columns, battlements, spires, and flying buttresses were mingled in the strangest confusion. On the tops and at the bases of most of the cliffs grew pine trees, some of considerable height, and the sand gave everything a clean, white look. Altogether it was as fantastically beautiful a place as I have ever seen."*

*- Theodore Roosevelt, circa late 1880's*

**OVER THE YEARS JOHN WESLEY'S BECOME** uncommonly familiar with "the strangest confusion," a situation apparently exacerbated by several years of specious over-indulgence and a sometimes road weary, peripatetic existence. Not really along the theme of "If this is Tuesday it must be Beruit," but more along the wavering line of "If this is 2016 can it possibly be Dawson City, Yukon?' or "What did I do to make them all go away forever?" or even as in this early October case "Is that really North Dakota over there?" And even more to the thoughtful point, the deal is more like his mind is a bicameral entity that wanders back and forth from third person to first while some aloof part of him sits back and watches the two cerebral chambers battle things out – "I want to do this" from one side and "No, he said he'd do this" from the other like a devious author shifting viewpoints within a narrative …

… I've wandered the southeastern corner of Montana many times, but I'd never made it to Medicine Rocks State Park located south of Baker and just north of Ekalaka on State Hwy 7. And yes that land of so many rude jokes was lying off on the short grass prairie a few air miles east of us – North Dakota, a much-maligned place of damn good country. I first came here looking for the power and vision the original visitors claimed that they'd found – some sort of internal truth that I knew that I didn't have anymore or, if I did, that centering buzz was buried so deep within me, hiding as it feared for its ethereal life behind piles of manufactured personality bullshit, that finding anything of value would be like rummaging through the local landfill down by Chester.

I'd drive in on a dusty, sandy road that was undergoing some serious construction by the boys from Baker. Twisting and turning through spacious stands of old Ponderosa the curious sandstone formations described by Roosevelt more than a century ago flash into view like large escapees from a twisted carnival traveling show then disappear just as quickly as we drop down an arc dip in the road only to be replaced by an even more fantastic shape. This geologic contrariness continues for perhaps a healthy mile until we break free of the trees and came upon a vista of dozens of the eroded shapes resting like long-ago wrecked ships on the native grass prairie that is glowing in autumn shades of yellow-gold, tan, purple-grey, still-brilliant green and rust. Beyond the formations the grasslands stretch for miles towards a horizon whose limits are marked by a soft blue sky that shimmers electric white near the ground. The day is cool, in the forties, and rafts of dark clouds sailed eastward.

I'd find a nice place to camp near a pair of the medicine rocks that had been heartily defaced with graffiti that ran to Jimmy adores Trish – 1996 and encircled by a crude heart. Some artiste has taken some serious time to carve a horse head replete with flowing main, but most of the scars are of the former variety. I wonder how many of these no doubt soulful relationships flourish to this day, but quickly turn addled with the enormity of the question, so I opt for a Jim Beam and ice. Coolers are arranged, sleeping gear settled, wood gathered and a fire built. I grill some brats and potatoes, have a few drinks and watch stars show up between the boiling masses of clouds. Despite the cold that threatens winter I feel energized, the lethargy and slight depression of simple-minded existence now vanished.

Medicine Rocks is a good, strong place and it's easy to understand high plains warriors and hunters of the Northern Cheyenne gathering here to draw on what this place offers. Hell, I was ready to jump in the Suburban, drive to New York and battle a few editors, but I fell asleep instead.

According to *Roadside Geology of Montana* the Medicine Rocks were originally part of a sea of ancient sand dunes. This is indicated by cross beds in the structures and the fact that the sand grains are small and of uniform size. The rocks appear to be the remains left by wind erosion since there are no stream channels in the area and each of them stands in a small depression much like the hollow left around a tree in heavy, wind-driven snowfall. The area is located on the

Ekalaka syncline which is a trough folded into layered rocks. As with much of this country, gas and oil is prevalent. We catch slight tastes of the stuff on the ever-present wind. Many of the rocks have eroded into a Swiss cheese-like appearance and a number of birds make their homes in these hollows, including a falcon that screeches, threatens with outstretched wings and puffed up breast and before eventually flying off somewhere each time he walks out onto the grasslands to be among the formations.

On this trip he'd originally planned on heading down south of Ekalaka to explore the Chalk Buttes but wound up spending five days here. With the weather turned warm the second day and the sun changing the colors and textures of the countryside as it passed across the sky he just never moved on. The whiskey and a dose or two of mescaline triggered and drove serene and lazy visions run riot with color and diaphanous vibration captivated for timeless hours as the planet spun and the sun appeared and disappeared on natural whim. The more time he spent here the more the land opens up in subtle shifts of color, light, texture and sound. Basic green of grass becomes multi-hued. Wind moving through pine limbs grows from a single lonely note to chords of song. No one else camped here during my five-day stay. The only people he spoke with were the guys from the road crew who came down to check me out, no doubt stunned by the fact that some clearly stoned Bozo from out of country would like their piece of turf so much that he would spend a number of days here doing not much of anything but walking, talking to himself, eating, and sleeping. Being a fisherman he queried the men about fishing in the area and they said that many of the ranch ponds were filled with rainbows. Seeing my eyes light up, they offered to get him onto to some of the water. He noticed on the drive in that many of these waters were, clear, relatively deep and surrounded with cattails and reeds. Prime stuff. He told them that he'd take them up on the offer next time Gill drifted over this way and they smiled, adding that the bird hunting for pheasants and sharptails was "not too shabby" either, closing with the clincher - antelope, mule and white-tail deer lived here, also.

Coming into Baker one day John Wesley spotted a pair of Zebras, which caused a pair of triple-takes and a near collision with a tractor. Was this the mescalito playing with his head? Jim Beam DTs? He'd learned from the road crew that the owner of that land has other exotics and the guys refer to it as a "petting zoo." He had a vision of bringing a Vermont friend of his who'd spent a good deal of time in Africa out this way, but wondered if the anomalous site would cause him to stroke out. He never got the chance to find out. Cancer killed him a few years back. Hate that shit.

He spent long hours feeding the fire both during the day and night, holding long discussions with himself talking about not much of anything or just cruising in place surrounded by the peace and strength of this place – John Wesley talking to another voice called Gill and Gill talking to a voice named John Wesley. By the end of the third night He'd regaled His various personalities, even the violent one, with enough scintillating anecdotes about his career as a sportswriter for a small-town daily in Wisconsin many years ago that Gill was forced to hide the Beam for his own well-being. And he never does get to tell all of the internal voices about that one infamous night with the Milwaukee Brewers' slugger Gorman Thomas at a place called The Pieces of Eight in Milwaukee. Next time.

One of his favorite books on the state is *The WPA Guide to 1930s Montana*. Thumbing through the ragged volume one afternoon he learns that Ekalaka (alt. 3,031) was originally called Puptown and began as a deadfall (saloon) for cowboys. Claude Carter, the town founder, a buffalo hunter and bartender, was on his way to another building site when his horses balked at pulling his load of logs through a mud hole at the current townsite. "Hell," Carter said, "any place in Montana is a good place to build a saloon. He built the Old Stand, which in a newer incarnation still stands and now offers good burgers and decent drinks. He knows having made the fifteen-minute drive for the repast each day a little before noon.

By day three he was a regular greeted with "What will it be Wes?" and a bourbon ditch arrived by drunken magic followed by a burger a few minutes later without John Wesley saying a word. His kind of place. Home on the road as The New Riders of the Purple Sage used to say a few decades ago. He'd kill decent chunks of time drinking and thinking about not much of anything or watching sports on TV. Gill had forgotten how much he liked Australian Rules Football, a delightful circus of unrestrained mayhem both on the field and in the stands. And he'd shoot the breeze with local ranchers and the bartender. He'd become accepted to the point where hunting game birds in the area was an option and so was casting poppers to bass in nearby ranch ponds. Maybe he'd move here. This country as good as any he's wandered in Montana and that's saying one hell of a lot.

Ekalaka was named for a Sioux girl called Ijkalaka (swift one) who was a niece of Sitting Bull. She was the best at breaking camp and so acquired her name. In 1875 David Harrison Russell, the first white homesteader in the region, married Ijkalaka, and in 1881 brought her to the community that had sprung up around the Old Stand. She lived in Ekalaka until her death in 1901. The town is home to a museum that has on display many remains and fossils of dinosaurs discovered in the region along with samples of a long-gone swampland forest now preserved in the form of petrified rock.

During the warm, sunny afternoons he wandered through the Ponderosa and among the rocks. He climbed over a rusty barbed-wire fence and walked across about a half-mile of prairie to a large formation covered in pines. The rock stands by itself on the southern edge of the park. From the top Gill could see for miles. Ekalaka was visible. Timbered buttes with wide valleys twist away between them stretching to the south and east. The crests of the Chalk Buttes, holding secret pockets of medicinal herbs an anthropological friend in the know about such things once told him, were visible as muted green and ochre in the haze of distance. Red-tailed hawks and a golden eagle rode the thermals. Black-capped chickadees bounced among the bushes. Wild roses hung with thick clusters of orange-red rosehips. Woodpeckers hammered on nearby trees in search of insects. A few late-season grasshoppers clacked as they bounded from grassy clumps to sun-exposed rocks. The clouds disappeared without my noticing, replaced by a soft but deep blue sky. The multi-colored grasses swayed sensuously in the wind in waves of motion that flowed eastward like a vast golden-tan river or circled along gentle rises that created large eddies of spinning air.

Thirty years ago this place probably would have bored John Wesley after a few hours. No classy trout streams. No jagged, snow-capped mountains. Only open-ended freedom and very few people. Now Medicine Rocks seems like country He'd like to live near. Good country. No cities.

Walking out onto the prairie and the isolated formations he watches as the sun sets casting a glow behind the rocks that moves from yellow to orange to blood red then fades to blue going indigo. A thin streamer of clouds reflects the last of the day's light in the same colors only fifteen minutes later.

The final night he grills a couple of ribeyes (damn hungry for some reason) and some corn-on-the-cob. Chocolate-chip cookies completed the meal. Then in the darkness he rebuilds the fire to a decent blaze and sits back. Gill looks at several of his psychotic personalities (aren't they all for all of us in our rare moments of honest evaluation) as they leaned over the fire rubbing their hands for warmth, worked on drinks or poked at the coals with long sticks that flared from their tips. "Did I ever tell you about the time Gorman ..." They looked up and shook their heads in unison saying "No more, please. God, no more." One of them rounds up our cups with barmaid skill, races to the picnic table, builds stiff drinks, hands Gill his, throws some wood on the fire and sits down in the long, dry grass. The moment's consciousness vanishes. He is unable to continue.

Soon bright white light began to illuminate the trees behind him. The Ponderosa and the Medicine Rocks cast deep shadows. All of us, even the violent one who normally preferred to be by himself, walk to the top of a nearby rise and watch as an enormous silver moon climbs above North Dakota. The light is intense, drowning out most of the stars. It climbs quickly into the sky, seeming to shrink in size but gain in intensity as it does so. The stars come back. A faint, green glow of Northern Lights moves up and down the horizon beyond Baker. Then a brilliant, bright green flickering startles us in the west. We turn and watch as a meteor low in the sky sizzles towards the Borealis. Pieces of the space rock broke off in miniature replicas of dazzling green. Gill imagines the sound of the thing streaking hundreds of miles an hour towards an earthly impact. Then the meteor is gone leaving behind the moon and the stars. Coyotes break into excited yipping and howling. They like the show, too.

The Medicine Rocks reveals itself over time, as it continues to do each time John Wesley returns. An electric friend filled with mysterious and wise depth. The longer he stays the more he sees. A special place in nowhere.

Gill wanders off into the dark thinking about long-ago high times when he was pretending to go to college in Missoula, maybe studying the arcane and rarely properly-taught subject of creative writing, certainly not at UM back then. Hell, the only time he ever saw his faculty advisor - a marginally talented clown who made a living sucking on the university tit, writing cover blurbs for other writers' books and occasionally publishing some turbid ramble about living in the West either in book form or as an article in some obscure periodical – was when the guy tried to bum cigarettes off of him in Eddie's Club or the East Gate Lounge. Gill always said he was out of smokes, ordered another shot then lit a Camel straight as he moved to the other end of the bar. He remembers a party after a Paul Butterfield and his Better Days Blues Band concert at the student union, a party where two enormous Blackeet were coupling naked in the doorway making entrance to the fete difficult. Once John Wesley surmounted this charming, romantic obstacle he found himself smoking reefers and drinking whiskey with the band's lean, brilliant and deep-voiced guitarist. They'd hook up again through sheer coincidence or is that synchronicity (doesn't matter) decades later along the Castle River in Alberta, each remembering the other almost at once. Such is life and happenstance. And he remembers a wild party at an old rodeo arena outside of Missoula. **acid rodeo** its own voice came to him ...

> *... the first good day of spring*
> *in the mountains*
> *and we all got*
> *ripped on acid*
> *with whiskey chasers*
> *here and there*
> *some bands were playing at*
> *an abandoned rodeo arena*
> *and somehow*
> *we got there*
> *without hitting*
> *any hallucinations*
> *we each bought a pitcher*
> *and waded through the beer soaked dirt*
> *a few cops*
> *and thousands of people*
> *tripping their brains out*
> *under a clear sky*
> *things turned crazy*
> *as they always do*
> *even the mountains*
> *made a statement or so*
> *just to keep things in perspective*
> *the bands came and went*
> *and the crowd*
> *was gone*
> *the wind came up*
> *and blew away*
> *it was wild*
> *Doug Kershaw and topless women*
> *and a bass player hit in the face*
> *with a jug of Oly*
> *never missing a beat*
> *when the music stopped*
> *we climbed in a pickup*

*for the ride back to town*
*four wheel drive this time*
*over the top of a Cadillac*
*roof crushed down*
*we kept going*
*to a bar*
*late and fluorescent bright*
*scrambled eggs and fried brains*
*shots of whiskey and*
*another rodeo down the drain ...*

# CHAPTER 4
## A Whole Lot of Nothing

**HE'D FINISHED THIS ONE** while drinking coffee before dawn that wound all the way through a wired orange, gold, pink sunrise. The words, the small story they told, remind him some of some hard times broke, real drunk and real alone in a dive hotel up Livingston way. Money showed up in the form of book royalties to bail him out of the small-time hell, but he can never forget those months, those terrible bleak, grey images. He called this one **the way it always was** ...

*time jags*
*not a lot of change*
*a bunch of noise*
*living in the back*
*old crumbling porch*
*the clown across the road*
*hammers new high rises*
*filled with secondhand crap*
*masquerading as style*
*drinking cheap wine*
*being twenty*
*seems possible*
*though*
*up front counts*
*where's money success acceptance*
*old mountains ask*
*cutthroats fin beneath shadowy banks*
*laughing in fish talk*
*another language unknown*
*gibberish spoken here*
*at least hangovers*

*feel right*
*images shimmer wander and roll*
*but retain crystal clarity*
*faces scream by*
*madder than hell*
*aware of conditions*
*motion lags behind thought*
*in these them those*
*pleasant situations*
*one day chases another*
*pretty much the same*
*wrapped in different years*
*variations on a theme*
*worn ragged ...*

... but times were better now and Mary Chapin Carpenter is riffing with gentle energy about Halley's Comet as Gill rolls down a red dusty road that cuts through early-May, thigh-high emerald grass on the Tongue River plateau. Wyoming's substantial Bighorn Mountains and Montana's lesser Pryors hang out silvery purple and snow crested white far to the west under a plain old high plains blue sky. Not a vault of impossibly perfect blue, whatever that is. And certainly not cerulean or indigo. Vault, impossibly and similar hackneyed words drove Gill crazy. "Why don't the lame bastards take up selling used cars," he'd mutter. "All they're selling now is dead end crap anyway." and certainly not cerulean or indigo. Just common blue. More than good enough. Pretty as it is. A few puffy clouds drift overhead no doubt on contract with the powers that be for this daytime shift. But the main player is the grass flowing along beside John Wesley. When he stops here and there to enjoy this spring afternoon the motion of all the green makes him think that he's moving, that his old rig is still rolling along. The only proof that he's somewhat motionless is the absence of a salmon-colored dust cloud trailing behind in a diminishing stream.

Halley's Comet is coming around again through the speakers after an 84-year absence and Gill negotiates a 120-degree corner that rises gradually all the way. He glances to his right out the passenger window. A bunch of antelope (pronghorns if you must) is keeping pace with him, sliding along at 30-35 mph, white bellies and tan legs invisible in the grass. The animals seem to be floating on the surface of the tall stems like miniature sloops working downwind on the sea. He punches replay. He likes Emmylou, this celestial tune. The antelope never even glance in John Wesley's direction but move in synch about 20 feet away. When the road sweeps left, so do they. And when he rolls along a casual stretch of straight flat road, so do they. The antelope are along for the ride – theirs and his. They're enjoying the day, the always new-found freedom of spring arrived again and the pure fun of being able to move so swiftly and gracefully over the high prairie. The song lasts a bit over three minutes, the volume is up and they must hear it, because when it ends they ease off away from the Suburban, eventually vanishing beyond a far swale. Here then gone.

He stops in the middle of what is now a dirt two-track, works his way to the back of the car, opens the doors, lifts the cooler lid, grabs a couple of cans of beer, opens them, takes long pulls and enjoys the low-eighties madness of putting another winter far away. The only sound is the wind pushing through the grass in a steady, rasping rush. So much green that even the air around him seems slightly tinted, glowing with the softest of green hue.

He thinks nothing about the antelope. No need to. The animal is part of this day, a part of the landscape that drifts past in enormous, barely perceptible swells of timelessness. A coyote emerges from the needle grass (He thinks that's what this is, but he's still working on the difference between bull trout and Dolly Vardon not to mention the various species of fir trees so firm identifications of a good deal of his natural world are often haphazard) about one-hundred yards ahead, begins crossing the road, looks at him, barks a couple of brief, laughing notes, lips curled up in a canine grin, head shaking, then the guy raises a hind leg and marks a clump of sage before wandering out of sight in the greenness on the far side. The grass shifts from the previously-mentioned emerald to dark green to almost quicksilver as it plays with the wind and the sun. This motion and colorful motion is hypnotic, intoxicating. Thirty minutes pass before he climbs back in the old rig and continue towards the drop that winds like a sunning rattlesnake to the Tongue River. There are carp to catch and maybe a rogue rainbow or two, and possibly, just possibly, and he quickly realizes that the limits of credulity are being stretched to the limits here, a brown trout. But remember, spring is a time of infinite possibility, even miracles.

~ ~ ~

For Gill spring is about the new, bright green grass with wildflowers adding their gleeful designer accents, and new leaves on the trees, and the pines turning from a black shade of frozen of this color to a green that glows, shimmers with life. Even hardcore lowlifes like the junipers, light up for a month or so. This is not a time for dredging up memories of past mistakes and evil doings. There are long, brutally cold winter nights filled with whiskey for that. April and May also bring on some fishing. Nothing like he used to do when psychotically flinging a fly everyday starting in late February passed for a driven good time. Now the fishing comes when it wants to and he catches fewer fish. More often than not they are catfish and carp and smallmouth bass, the fish of his youth. Though trout are targeted, also.

John Wesley looks off into the distance while relighting a Marsh Wheeling cigar that went cold during the beginnings of his reverie.

Another spring. Another part of Montana. The day is like the one above with more wind and larger clouds (this bunch must have a better contract). Working up against the relatively warm current, the backside grasses all but blot out the sky and the sandy yellow and grey cutbanks. Hills covered with the muted green of new sage round off the horizon. The grass is over his head. The new green of small willow bushes clings thickly beside the moving water. The yellow-green of cottonwoods rises above me. The neon greens of aquatic grasses swing and wave in the current at his feet and as fair ahead as he can see. Gill casts a large brown Elk Hair caddis between the seams of grass because he sees bugs that look like my fly rise off the surface - matching the hatch with technical subtlety.

The smallmouth are eager, unsophisticated or perhaps they're buzzed on the new season like he is. John Wesley lands a bunch of the bass in a couple of hours – none of them large, most of them small, eight inches or so. They fight well. They are much stronger than trout inch for inch. A 12-inch bass smacks the Elk Hair, then rips upstream bending the rod abruptly struggling like a two-pound cutthroat. The fish zips into the weeds, twists the line and with a shake of its head, snaps the tippet. He admires its tactic expertise. He can do this all afternoon and probably will, but for now, he edges over in the knee-deep water and sits on the bank in thick grass that surrounds him like a bower. The thick stems and wide leafy tops brush back and forth against his shirt, his face. Gill feels like he's being caressed before realizing that he's been on the road alone a few days past healthy.

Quartering upstream and across the creek from him is a long spit of exposed sandy soil marked with serpentine strips of blue-green shading darker with black miniature slashes. One of the strips moves and coils. Gill thinks rattlesnake. He always thinks rattlesnake, even the one time he saw a red, white and black milk snake alongside a game trail in the Missouri Breaks. His hands shake as he pulls a small pair of binoculars from a pocket. Focusing in Gill sees that there are seven or eight snakes enjoying the sun like bathers on a Riviera beach. He expects to hear strange French pop music coming from radios resting beside bottles of tanning potions. Perhaps this is a topless beach, he wonders. Way too far gone. It's back home tomorrow or maybe on to the Milk River. What's the difference at this point in the proceedings. The serpents reveal themselves to be common garter snakes out for a day at the beach. He relaxes, finishes his sandwich and works up the creek through the watery plants swirling around my legs. He spies a large smallmouth, maybe 16 inches, crash the surface as it crunches an early-season hopper. Changing to a Joe's Hopper Gill closes in.

~ ~ ~

Springs are all of this spinning within the flashback-memoried emeralds. That's the color in the head when this time of year comes to mind. No fancy-named items, just emerald green.

John Wesley's been on the road now for a couple of weeks and visions of his home landscape ride in on him coming from the middle of nowhere with uncommon brilliance and clarity.

And what spring would be complete without a lazy drive around and through the Sweet Grass Hills in early

May. Along wide dirt and gravel roads, up rocky cuts and over barely discernable lanes, all of these paths slipping through lush fields of grass that smell of water, the wind, the earth, living. Evenings of slight breeze that moves all of it in a gentle hissing so soft it feels like a dream not quite remembered while thousands of rainbows break the surface of a small lake thirty feet below; or lurching past an old gold-mining operation the road suddenly clears the site and opens to an expanse of green that shifts and elongates far into Alberta, the Cypress Hills a mere suggestion off to the northeast, ranch ponds flickering silver, gold and copper in the sunset glow, the air cool as it drifts down from the top of Middle Butte, the grass now holding and twisting with yellows, reds, oranges.

Or maybe afternoons cruising along old highways around Lennep, Lingshire or perhaps Checkerboard and watching the cattle and horses graze on the luxuriant grasses in the lower meadows as ranchers move from irrigation ditch to irrigation ditch directing the flow of precious water from one field to the next in vain attempts to prolong their landed greenness forever. Days of hundreds of miles and shifting light that end too soon and are always remembered. There are lots of these.

Times of rounding a curve cutting through the Judith Mountains a couple of hours before sunset after rocking through a lunatic thunderstorm of purple clouds, white lightning that sizzled, thunderclaps that slammed through the windows, rain so intense the wipers freaked, then hail. Now the sun shows as the weather struts east to raise some trouble over Grass Range way and eventually the Breaks and lonesome Jordan. Rays of light slice through the dregs of the storm clouds and turn the emerald grass brilliant, into colors Gill's never seen. And just for the hell of it an intense rainbow arcs from somewhere above down into the forest somewhere at the base of the mountains. The prismatic display radiates, grows hotter as though the whole damn countryside is saying, "Now look at your emerald." And he does. Permutations, exotic and alien shadings of the color drift, mix and fluoresce all over the place creating an image of a land that is both new and beyond ancient. This free-flowing gem stone countryside, his private jewel right now, is part of an infinite dance flashing and winking within the light.

Man, this is magic for a jaded freak.

~ ~ ~

This time of the year, this place, out here by himself, all of it combines to form an atmosphere of total aloneness. This is not a mood of loneliness or a desire to seek out the comradeship of my fellow humans. Nothing that drastic or even morose. Only the feeling of being totally by myself, with no one else around or even to consider for these few days of dwindling brilliance.

Now is October. Everything about the day looks as Montana in October should on this sunny, blue sky afternoon. The aforementioned blue is deep. The light breeze with its swirling mixture of warm and cool is familiar. The scent of dried-out sage, lightly pungent and earthy is condign. The shades of dead grass rocking easily on the wind like an old man sitting on his front porch remembering years past while sipping coffee grown cool with the driftings of memory are as they should be. The colors range from flat tan through silvery yellow and on into a weathered golden patina the finish of well-used metal. A Western meadowlark calls out, not with the exuberance of spring and the promise of warm months, but with the voice of a creature that knows hard times are coming and that a day like this one is money in the bank. A pair of antelope work across a rising fold in this flat maybe a mile away. They winded me as soon as I topped the slope, maybe earlier, and are working without nervousness away and soon over the rise. Several ravens follow the river's course as it flows north towards Northern Cheyenne country. Light glistens off black, moving wings. They squawk and caw among themselves, but the distance mutes the conversation to a barely real level.

Camp is a few miles behind. Gill is walking along this bench looking for a couple of sharptails that maybe he can drop for dinner. Whether he's successful or not doesn't matter. The walking with his late stepfather's twenty-gauge Beretta is what counts. Whenever he does this all of the fine times he and Ken had together chasing fish and birds return. He relives these without any awareness of specific moments, only an overall awareness of days well spent with a good friend.

That's all this afternoon spent pushing across this bench is about. He doesn't expect to kick up anything. The simplicity of the colors is good. The blue, gold, browns, buff, ochre, charcoal and salmon in the cliffs rising above him on the east, the different blue of the river far away and below, the fading green clinging to life along the stream's banks, all of this makes sense because it doesn't have to. John Wesley appreciates this wild simplicity.

Twenty feet in front from out of a tall bunch of grass four large grouse lumbers up about six feet then starts to beat down with the wind. He sees tan, grey, buff and yellow feathers. Sage grouse. Wings beat rapidly as the birds shout *kuk-kuk-kuk-kuk*. Then they glide swooping near ground level before the beating begins again. The gun is at his shoulder reflexively. Gill locks in on the bird ahead of the bead at the end of the barrels, dark brown spikes of its tail feathers aimed at him in a futile defense. An easy shot as images from past autumns merge with the fleeing bird …

… past 8,000 feet, many miles above the primitive campground at less than 6,000, hanging out beneath a battered group of storm-blown pine trees. The river Gill wants to fish is 1,000 feet below, the trail slippery, vertiginous, deadly. Lightning, wind, rain, hail blow all over the place. He thinks that he should have stayed at his dry camp in the Tongue instead of running down the Interstate into Wyoming and up into the climbing tilted slabs of country that are the Middle Fork of the Powder River.

There are fish way down there. Browns and rainbows that maybe are fished over once every couple of years in this remote stretch. For now there's no safe way to reach them. As he checks the trailhead three mule deer slip and clatter past him, making remarkable four-hooved-off-the-ground-at-once leaps to the side to avoid running into the startled man. John Wesley inches down the path on his butt. Everything seems to drop away hundreds of feet down to broken rock, sage, tangled brush, matted grass and cactus. In less than one-hundred yards of slipping on the greasy surface he comes to where the deer stopped and made their turn around. If they won't go further, he won't either. The view slanting down across sere though damp grasslands gives way to the walls of the opposite side of the canyon. Red, ochre, bluish-grey, pink, the black of a coal seam spin in and out of view as the weather hammers the high country with what will surely be the first snowstorm of the year. What was seventy degrees at noon is freezing now.

Back at camp he touches off some charcoal in his Little Smoky grill, opens a cheap bottle of Merlot (he's brought more than several), pulls on a sweater then a wax cotton poncho and wool hat. The grill is positioned on the lee side of the Suburban. So is his chair. The small blaze casts sufficient warmth. The wine tastes okay. Hell it comes with a cork. Must be good. He's wrapped a sliced potato with onions, butter, salt and coarse black pepper in foil and buried it in the coals. A ribeye will follow soon. Gill will survive.

A Cuban cigar, a gift from a friend months ago, after dinner with some more wine sounds reasonable.

Dark, rolling clouds, lots of lightning and thunder that crashes like it's right behind him. Close enough that when the wind is down Gill can feel the compression of the air caused by the detonation push on my eardrums and brush his cheeks. The land way up this way is wild – no people, buildings, lights - made even crazier by the weather. Snow is falling as the thunderstorm plays on. This is great. The steak sizzles. Then he eats before putting things in order. He opens some more wine, lights the cigar and enjoys the evening in his solitude surrounded by so much of what's kept him alive all this time. Eventually he crawls into his sleeping bag resting on top of a foam pad covered with a quilt in the back of the rig. True luxury that would be considered ostentatious by his years-ago persona.

In the morning he rises. A foot of snow has turned the landscape blinding intense bright in the sunrise. Orange blinding wandering to blaze yellow into silver and then just white hot blinding. He snacks on some fruit and bagels, loads the gear and prepares to head back down in four-wheel – slippery but easily doable. Checking around for anything left behind as always, a good habit among a number of bad ones, he realizes that the Little Smoky is not around. The wind swiped his friend of hundreds of fires in the dead of night in places far away from anywhere. Scatters of ash from last night's cooking mark the snow to the cliff's edge. Grabbing his binoculars he follows the awful trail. Easing to the precipice he lies down in the snow and scans the terrain below.

There.

Down on a ledge several hundred feet is the Little Smoky. In the glasses he sees that the handle is mashed into the lid's surface. The main part of the grill is mangled, twisted, bent beyond recognition.

Lord, life is hell sometimes and he remembers killing large animals like deer, antelope, elk and others with sadness and regret that grows as the years pass but he can't stop the killing. He says a brief prayer, walks back to the Suburban and drives somberly back down to the low country that is shadow flashing red sand and yellow dirt snowless beneath the partly cloudy sunlight way off by Kaycee ...

... crawling up the narrow two-track just this side of the North Dakota border Gill pauses in front of a rusting barbed wire gate. He unlatches the thing and pulls it across the road so that he may pass. The wire and tree limb posts make a muffled scratching noise on the ground. Even in the silvery light of a full-moon night he can see that the tall dying grasses appear flaxen, a slight silvery blond like he's imagined Harry Morgan's wife's hair looked after she had it dyed in a Havana beauty parlor to please her husband in *To Have and Have Not*. After driving through the gate he closes it and walks back to the Suburban. The dust puffs around his moccasins along the path. The powder feels soft, giving.

Climbing and coming around a sharp, Ponderosa-lined bend the sandstone rock formation that he's come to rises starkly against the sky like some ancient monument with a large bell-shaped crown capping the structure nearly dead center. The rock that was forced up by unimaginable force millions of years ago is eroding from wind and rain. Crenellations, holes, spires and parapets stand out in moonlight relief, the features growing more distinct as he draws closer and the moon rises higher in the sky.

He stops on a gentle rise that looks across a broad depression to the natural sculpture from what appears to be equal footing. This is an illusion created by distance and the night, but feels like he's standing level with the bell. The air is warm and moves through the grass and trees with a faint hiss. Nighthawks boom above. A bird he doesn't know makes a persistent cry that sounds like a phonograph needle riding on vinyl that goes around and around at the end of a record, perhaps *Let It Bleed*. The land grows brighter as does this formation beneath the persistent moon. Most of the stars are overcome, made invisible by this radiance. Coyotes howl to the south in the direction of not-so-distant Wyoming. In the morning he'll be able to see the northwestern edge of the South Dakota Black Hills one-hundred miles away. For now John Wesley sits on a smooth boulder and enjoys the fall night ...

... and watches a vaporous image that gains form as seconds move by sliding across high plains that used to be always dark out at night was easy. The roads are still straight at one hundred miles an hour and in some circles running this quickly is even accepted behavior. What better way to chase down a starlight mystery within wild emptiness that never needs filling, but is being smothered in a neon avalanche, a vastness that now glows bleakly in gathering locations like a prairie Vegas full of losers crapped out on dead dreams. A certain dirt road is hard to find, but cautious navigation scares up friendly desolation - rare places unseen, connected by undefined space. Standing up here on this old eroded rock dome looking down he smiles at the knowledge that there's still spaced out darkness, quiet, sanity ...

... now the sage grouse is moving away from him but remaining the same size in his vision. Gill swings the Beretta with and slightly ahead of the bird and squeezes the trigger. The golden grass ripples in sharp focus against the blue horizon ...

... John Wesley walks after his shot to the now still grouse.

### hail

*darkness is always open*
*some things are rarely there*
*like rolling along beside a river*
*with a friend*
*and up ahead*
*what is frightening*
*boils and swirls*
*in the sky*
*whipping dead brown hills*
*with its anger*
*and then pounding away*
*with mean intent*
*destroying the ability to see*
*hammered into anxious fear*
*and all anything living*
*can do or wants to do*
*is run frantically from hell*
*find shelter and hide*
*and maybe try again*
*later*

# CHAPTER 5

## Visual Distortions

### caribou crazy

*spend a lot of time looking*
*for things standing*
*right out front*
*happens often in the Rockies*
*searching for caribou comes to mind*
*they are right*
*where they are*
*a hell of a lot of them*
*standing deep in a stream*
*chasing little cutthroats*
*feeling the casual pressure of eyes*
*caribou on the near shore*
*grazing thoughtful soundless*
*look at water for awhile*
*everything seems to flow*
*caribou are like this*
*gliding uphill*
*through the trees*
*and gone*
*back again through time*

**THE FOLLOWING MINOR TALE** is a compilation of a bunch of things John Wesley experienced over a run of about 10 years. As he rolled down the road he thought about many incidents in his life. These that follow are some of them. Everything in this number happened, but not in the short span of time covered by these thoughts. Northern Wisconsin is excellent country to play in, at least it was many years ago. His closest friend in high school parents owned a place on a birch-cloaked peninsula that jutted into a small lake holding walleye, smallmouth bass and muskies. The last species he admired for its swift, deadly killing and immense power. A killing machine marauding the depths. Of freshwater lakes in the North Country. John Wesley would stay with his friend at this place hiding in the forest between Boulder Junction and Presque Isle, an area that is considered by many to be the nexus of musky fishing. They'd fish at all hours of the day – at night for walleyes, early in the morning for muskies and they'd wade sandy shores casting to feeding smallmouths. Grouse, deer, lynx and black bear roamed the forest. Geese and ducks dropped in on their way north or south. Eagles and osprey roamed the airways. There were brook trout in really isolated little streams that flowed through and off the Shields country both in Wisconsin and the adjacent UP of Michigan. Those fish were colorful, wild and some of them were big. The days spent chasing all of this and then drinking beer and whiskey way into the night seemed like they had an eternal life. They didn't. His friend took his life while only in his mid-twenties with a shotgun, empty gin bottles scattered about his apartment, a blood-spattered bible on his lap, the book opened to Leviticus. John Wesley's never been back to this country since. His friend's death worked him over for many years, and still does to a minor extent, until he finally decided to write this story and the poem **caribou crazy**. When he finished he felt that much had been put in better places, that a large, ugly weight had been lifted and an emptiness had been at least partially filled. John Wesley moved on from this segment of his life. This is not to be confused with closure. He's learned that there is no such phenomenon, either in life or death. He called a friend who lives over near Townsend, and asked if he would consider publishing the story in a magazine he edited. A few days later he returned the call saying that he liked the story a good deal and would use it. That completed the circle, The story was called The Eternity Hunt ...

... The deer was down, an easy shot: the animal lying across a tiny spring creek that flowed over a duff of brown, grey and yellow birch leaves, pine needles and moss. After twenty-six months of hunting this one animal I thought the killing would leave me exhilarated, shaking, unable to walk. It didn't just then, though all of that would show up in force later that night. Walking up to the buck, reaching down and lifting its heavy head by the rack, the touch of a cold breeze on my face and the crystal sound of the moving water, none of this felt real. I thought that was surprising back then, but not today.

For someone unaccustomed or incapable of exhibiting patience in situations requiring stealth or the consummate nuances associated with tact, still-hunting whitetail deer in the woods or, for that matter, fly fishing for brown trout, and raising a family, can be fraught with absurdity, craziness and even a touch of layered insight. This realization made its first tentative appearance at Red Bass Lake that crisp, lonely October day in northern Wisconsin more than twenty years ago, the subtle shadings of meaning gleaned from the hunt are only now discernible as I stumble and lurch through the harsh honesty of my forties – the wear and tear of many years well and hard spent don't brook many lies. While I know a little bit more than I did then, that was the first time I understood the interrelatedness of seemingly random events. How a conversation here, falling down in a wet ditch there and taking the fork going that way all added up to right now. Heady stuff for an irresponsible hipster back then, and still a little scary today.

Reaching the point where earthly truths were revealed and a deer was actually killed was the tricky part, made all the more so by two factors: Inexperience as a hunter and cocksure idiocy. I planned to hunt whitetail somewhere in the birch, poplar and pine woods up near Presque Isle just below Michigan's UP. It looked easy in a state where not running into a deer for a period of two weeks while chugging to and fro on daily and nightly errands of little importance is almost impossible. The deer are everywhere, I was informed several nights running by the boys nursing their schooners of Chief Oshkosh at the Sportsman.

For me, local opinion was dead wrong. It simply didn't apply. True, like anyone else who had ever hunted deer in the state, there had been the brain-dead, easy hunts where I walked into an area I knew held deer and waited for the does and forkhorns to come gliding silently out from the woods to feed along the edge of a clearing and then I pulled the trigger. Before the hunt for the buck at Red Bass, I thought this was the game. Not anymore for me, even if it still is for others. The journey to get that one deer nearly finished me as a hunter before I even knew what that meant. Yet that solitary, long-distance stalk covering a raft of whirling seasons, in some maniacal, demented way drove the fever of the chase into me with barbed permanence.

I was familiar with the country around Presque Isle. Had been for years. A friend owned a place on a narrow peninsula jutting out into a small lake filled with walleye that later gave way to the ravenous attentions of muskies. The predators found their way into the water via a new culvert connecting with Red Bass Lake. The large metal tube bridged a soggy gap between the two waters providing an excellent food source for the muskies and a swift end to some fine walleye fishing. This was upsetting, but I quickly learned to take my fishing where and how I found it and the muskies of Red Bass were large, aggressive and wild. No one but my friend and I ever fished for them. There were too many famous waters – Turtle, Flambeau, Rainbow, Spirit River – for serious guides and fishermen to bother with obscure lakes like Red Bass. We'd hauled an old, battered Grumman canoe into the lake, stashing the noisy thing in some cattails that clogged a small cove. We had the place to ourselves along with the ruffed grouse, osprey, lynx and the deer.

Three years into college my friend ended his life with a twelve-gauge Merkel for his own sad reasons. No one wanted the gun. I was offered the piece but declined. Too weird for me, but I kept coming back to Presque Isle and Red Bass Lake, camping in the thick woods for days on end, catching large muskies on hideous-looking streamers tied on mean, long-shanked hooks and casting an old red-glass Fenwick fly rod. Or I'd spend the day walking through the trees or just sitting by a small fire. I loved the place, but now there was a sense of melancholy emptiness sliding across the surface of the lake. Years ago my friend and I had filled an empty gallon Everclear jug with pennies as a hedge against the time when we might run out of cash for burgers and beer. I'd retrieved that heavy jar and set it in the hollow of an old stump.

One day staring at the copper coins got the better of me. I filled my pockets with the things, bound and determined to head into town and have numerous memorial drinks to my friend. (A sad state of mind, but we all arrive here sooner or later.) Coat and jean pockets bulged with god-knows-how-many-pounds of the things. I lurched down the faint trail like Jacob Marley's ghost (or my friend's?) towards the truck.

Working up a slight rise, I tripped over a root, feel in a heap and rolled like a set of deranged barbells down into a wet, leafy gully, winding up face first in a rotting-black-mud bottomed creek bed.

Rising up on my elbows I thought "Oh shit. They'll love me at the tavern, especially with all of these damn pennies." I rolled over and out of the water. Lying on the ground looking uphill I saw the deer. A buck, its rack softly shining in the late-day sun, was looking at me, motionless, right foreleg frozen in mid-step. Moist black nose barely twitching, dark eyes focused, the creature appeared stunned at the bizarre scene sprawled before it. I craned my neck for a better view. This motion scared the deer. It turned and bounded away in one motion. On its flank I clearly saw a long, jagged scar, probably from a barbed-wire fence that resembled the electric bolt on the helmets worn by the San Diego Chargers.

Something clicked in a slow mind. If I could find a buck after falling down, shooting one standing up should be a piece of cake. The rack would look good on a wall and the meat would come in handy during the depths of another cash-poor winter. That was the ticket. I'd come back to this spot for this particular deer this fall. The boys at the bar, after they finished commenting on my appearance and offering various suggestions about what I could do with my pennies, thought this was a terrific idea. "Hell, you're already in full camo," they said in reference to my muddied visage. This set off a round of cackling, hacking and wheezing that seemed to last several days. Despite this encouragement, I knew I'd be back.

And I was for a couple of cool weeks in October and for ten miserable, sodden days in November. I never saw the buck. Sign was everywhere. Shiny, black pellets like immature Milk Duds lay scattered in piles along the serpentine trails on both sides of the little creek that was more ephemeral rivulet than honest flowing stream. And there were bunches of them in a small, sheltered area on top of the rise where wild berries grew in thick clumps. I found scrapes on birch and pine trunks where the buck had left his scent and gnawed on low-hanging boughs. There were places where his hooves had torn up the ground in what looked like a free-form, North Woods hockey game. His deep tracks turned the dirt alongside the creek into thick, gooey mud that smelled of gaseous rot, of decaying life. Not far from the lake, the creek widened into a clear pool maybe a foot deep by several feet in diameter. This was where he drank. The marks were distinct. Hooves spread wide as he bent down to the water, those prints were all around the pool. Why here I wondered? Less exposure to predators (mainly man, I imagined) than down at the lake? Whatever. This was a safe place tucked beneath the trees. Shelter. The area provided everything the deer would need. And I was obviously a minor and uncommon irritation or perhaps a passable form of entertainment.

I hunted hard those days. No, not hunted. I didn't know what that involved. The effort, concentration and commitment needed to even begin to think like a hunter eluded me, still does most of the time. I walked a lot learning the lay of this small piece of land. Not nearly as well as the deer, but much better than I ever thought possible. I spent long hours shivering in all the wrong places, though I did see plenty of grouse and the vanishing form of a wild cat, perhaps a lynx. But I never once saw the damned deer. All of the time I was convinced that he was nearby, watching, playing it close to the vest, waiting for me to move on.

The season closed and I almost called a halt to the proceedings, but something kept driving me, wouldn't let me give up. Maybe it was the spirit of my friend. Who knew? That winter I did plenty of reading and learned a little, especially from a book called *The Still-Hunter* by Theodore S. Van Dyke. Originally published in 1882, a first cursory reading showed that Van Dyke knew a good deal more about hunting than I did, than I ever would. The guy was driven. That was perhaps my first lesson. If you want to embrace anything wild you have to be willing to jump in all the way, to spend the time, to endure the discomfort. One thing in particular leaped off the page at me: I'd been a loud buffoon clanking and crashing around in the woods. I'd never had a chance with this buck. The next summer I'd learn his country much better. I'd find places to hide, to conceal my unnatural form. And I'd work at being quiet. Very quiet.

From June through September I scouted that land hard, learning every dip, rise, moist spot, downed tree, clearing and clump of bushes. I saw the buck twice. Both times at dusk, the animal always sliding away with swift, silent motion. He was larger now. At once there in my sight, then gone. I was convinced that I saw the jagged scar each time. Without that buck, the hunt was a dead issue. Another deer wouldn't do.

When the season opened I spent every spare moment, and there were many back then, walking those woods or holding tight beneath a large poplar or birch waiting for the buck. During midday I paddled the canoe around the lake casting streamers for muskies, big ones, over twenty-five pounds. The fish slammed the patterns. The red glass rod finally exploded from this stress in a spray of splinters when one of the fish ran, stopped, then tore across the surface shaking its head in a gill-rattling display of power. I needed a new rod, anyway. By the end of the season Red Bass was frozen over and so was I. One evening after a hot shower in my motel room – black-and-white TV, worn, chintz bedspread, "magic fingers" bed – I wandered up the hill to the tavern for a few drinks and a large, rare steak. I'd had enough. The buck had won. I'd stick to fish and grouse.

After dinner and a few more belts I struck up a conversation with an old boy who was always hunched over the bar working on shots of bar whiskey and a beer. He listened to my story of failure with little expression, sipping the booze and working on a long-necked Old Style. I managed to work in my successful musky exploits.

"Can't kill a damn buck stinkin' up the country the way you did," he said. Want that buck or a goddamned fish? Make your choice. You told me where he is and when he's going to be there," and he paused to fire up a Chesterfield. "Think the damn thing is stupid? You're up there banging around, probably along that little crick and burning wood in a smoky fire like some damned fool from Chicago. Make a lot of damn noise popping the tops to those beer cans, too, I'd imagine. Surprised the muskies didn't turn tail."

A long stare and then he went back to work on his drinks. I was dismissed, embarrassed, angered. I spent the winter, when I wasn't covering sports for the Beloit Daily News in the southern part of the state, thinking. Yeah, I'd think a lot in places like The Turtle Tap, The Zoo Gardens and Pinky's Pub. Next season things would be done right.

That summer I only visited the place twice to re-familiarize myself with the terrain and to see if I could spot the buck. I did on the second trip. He was standing on the rise above the creek in the fading, golden light of sunset. He was larger than ever. The scar had deepened, showing a rough, weathered brown surrounded by tan hair. He turned and looked at me. I said "This fall. This fall for sure. We both left.

On my way out to Red Bass Lake that fall I passed the sheriff's squad car pulled over on the gravel and brown grass along the side of the road. A man was slumped in the front seat, head bandaged. Blood had seeped through the layers of gauze. A county four-by-four was parked just behind, blue and red lights flashing. A handcuffed man was leaning against the Bronco. I stopped to see what was going on. The prisoner was my friend from the bar. Curious business here from the looks of things.

"What happened?" I asked.

"Jake shot the sheriff. He'll be all right, but he's real pissed right now. Give him plenty of room. I got his .357 away from him just in case. Jake's drunker than a skunk. Damn fool said he thought the light flashing off the squad car looked like horns," said the deputy as he headed over to the manacled hunter who was now sprawled on the ground. "Damn Jake used to be a hell of a hunter. One of the best in this country. Said he was going up to Red Bass to shoot some muskies or a big buck he knew about. I don't know which. He never makes sense anymore."

The deputy walked over to his wounded comrade, who was now stomping around and waving his arms while swearing creatively about hunters and where was his gun. He'd be okay. I looked at Jake. My pal from the bar. My mentor. The son-of-a-bitch was going to poach my turf. Couldn't trust anyone in this world. I climbed back into my truck and drove off wondering if this was a bad or a good omen. The rest of the ride to the buck's hold out was uneventful. The October sky was filling with dark clouds. There wasn't any wind. The forecast called for scattered showers later tonight. Nothing to sweat.

There was a perfect place to conceal myself just

across and below the small pool. The breeze moved downhill, downstream late in the day. No chance of being winded when the buck came out of cover to feed and drink. I sat motionless, hidden in the brush, had been since mid-afternoon. My back and knees ached, but I focused on the spot where I was trying to will the buck to appear forty yards above and through a gap in the birch and brush. He had to approach from there. My rifle was aimed in this direction, resting on my upraised knees and against my chest. All I had to do was sight and squeeze the trigger. Dusk approached and the light shaded down through gold to amber then pewter. Would he show? This time I knew that the answer was "Yes," but still had doubts about what I knew would be the inevitable sequence of this long-running deal.

Already looking through the scope at the gap, I saw the buck materialize. Empty sky one instant, then the animal's silhouette the next. I held my breath, aimed at the shoulder, exhaled slowly, and fired. The sound of the detonating round rocked the still forest. The buck dropped from view in the scope. I looked up and he was down. Motionless. Dead. The gunpowder smell was strong, pungent.

That was all there was to twenty-six months. This vision of the buck and his large rack. The sound of the rifle firing. The deer lying on the ground. The connection between my departed friend, the jar of pennies, falling in the mud and first seeing this buck, the talk with Jake at the bar, all of it, flashed through my mind, all of this noticed but not yet examined or appreciated. I did realize that I hated killing but need to participate in the act as much as a junkie needs his junk. I would examine this internal conundrum, too, but as I mentioned this too would come later. For now I had a deer to dress out.

~ ~ ~

So that's the story and here's another one that is something of an odd companion to the first and it's all pretty much true, just like it really happened, just some more mental road ramblings of John Wesley's ...

"...**WHAT'S THAT AWFUL SOUND, JOHN**?"
The one doing the asking was my girlfriend back then, the uncommon woman who suggested the poetry collection in the first place. And if you believe and are capable of shifting forward in linear time, she's now my wife, but that's a tale for another collection of ramblings and mentioned here purely for amusement's sake.

"Out To Lunch by Eric Dolphy."

"Very strange. Is the whole CD like this? Where's the melody?"

"It's in there somewhere and yes it is." I smiled at my companion who looked at me and decided to let the matter drop. Sixties alto sax. Discordant harmonies. Inverted rhythmic phrases. Admittedly Dolphy lacks the stylistic sophistication of the prodigiously talented Kenny G, but then our fishing trips never come close to reaching the rarefied levels of nuance and sophistication as do those delicate, foreign-wines-for-lunch, pampered float trips offered in the glitz ads that are scattered throughout the major fly fishing magazines like dead carp along a muddy bank - the excursions where you absolutely must wear fourteen-thousand bucks of clothing draped with zirconium-encrusted hemostats, stomach pumps, thermometers, and don ball caps plastered with catchy phrases like "I fish, therefore I am."

Perhaps that's an unfair, even harsh, line of thought, especially as we slide out of Augusta up a dusty road towards a place we like to fish and camp at along the Sun River. After all, we aren't running down esoteric central Montana trout water in my old beater pickup anymore, either. We sold out a couple of years back and bought an expensive Sports Utility Vehicle with leather seats and a real nice sound system. The Tahoe is now our only tangible asset, unless you figure in two hundred fly rods, camera gear, a .357 magnum and a bunch of jazz CDs. At least the rig's windshield is cracked and chipped, the body has a dent or two and the interior reeks of damp waders and soggy Triscuts creating an ambiance approaching that of the Ft. Peck Inn, a lofty vision in itself. None of this really matters, which is why I'm writing about it. The idea of the whole unplanned, undisciplined journey, the shaky premise we use to justify our inability to hold regular jobs or our very real need to get away from daily interactions with people, is that we live for good country and whatever is found there. And that by photographing and writing about our experiences with intensity and insight we can share the free-form energy and arcane experiences we encounter with others. And we can earn lots of money.

Just another line of bullshit we run by ourselves and scores of unwitting victims from Forsyth to the Port of Del Bonita in a vague attempt to legitimize the insanely good times we have out here in the middle of everywhere doing what ever zips into our heads.

Standing in the wetness of the cool Sun tossing a shredded hopper pattern out into the center of the river with a rhythm turned moronic through a deleterious combination of heat and repetitious casting is scintillating. To be sure, the casting is at once brilliant and artful with the line unfurling from its tight loop with unerring accuracy fifteen, twenty feet distant, but this is still repetitious, when out of the clear blue water comes a large chunk of determined silver, white mouth wide open. The fly is gone and the line on the reel is going, too. A rainbow leaps fifty yards from us, very large, and then falls back to the river and steals more line. The trout leaps again, as far above the water's surface as I've ever seen a freshwater fish go. And this time when the rainbow comes down, it does not drop down into the current, but, instead, flexes its tail flat on the top of the river and thrashes through a hot breeze fast away from me. Lifting gradually backwards on the rod to take up the slack I hear a sound that is a combination of crumpling Saran wrap and breaking stick matches. Something isn't right. I've lost control of the situation. A new experience. Nothing I do with the rod helps and then I look at the pricey piece of graphite. Broken. Shattered just above the handle. Four hundred bucks of junk and the trout throws the hook with bored disdain. The very large rainbow gleefully arcs through the light, jumping over and over as it heads down river. Pretty to watch. Tough to take, even at this advanced, broken-down stage in the life-long proceedings.

"Nice job, John Wesley," she says, always using my middle name for purposes of accentuating her sarcasm.

"Not my fault. The damn rod blew up. Cheap piece of crap. Damn good fish down the tubes."

"That's what you always say."

"What do you mean 'always?'"

"That makes five you've wrecked so far and it's not even August. Thank God for Uncle Orvis."

"Thank God, nothing. I think I've been disinherited."

"What'd you do this time, darlin?"

"I quit drinking and they don't like the way I dress," and I lit a Camel to ease the pain.

"What's wrong with the way you dress?"

There is nothing like the support and compassion of a good woman to steer you through tough times. I begin to trudge back to camp to grab another rod, her laughter rings in my always ringing ears. I start to laugh. Hell, the things have a lifetime guarantee and there are at least fourteen more in the back of the car. Break one. String up another. Onward and upward.

Speaking of which, I look upriver and pray that the ancient, leaking cement structure lyrically known as Gibson Dam, a decrepit edifice that blocks the Sun a couple of miles away hangs on for at least another few days. The idea of being washed away by billions of gallons of unleashed reservoir water, the two of us entwined in a confused jumble of sleeping bags and impaled by tent stakes, all this as we plummet one-hundred-and-fifty feet over the diversion dam roaring a quarter-mile just below us, the image holds little wonder or excitement for me. A couple of divorces, several addictions, numerous intriguing conversations with law enforcement officials and an awfully clear awareness that big money ain't in my future are all the thrills I want for this ride. Then again ... if I were killed in such a dramatic mishap ... maybe my books would sell.

Mid-morning a few days later and the Rocky Mountain Front screams at us from fifty miles away. The outraged mountains dominate our vision with a barrage of intense purple, white, salmon, slate grey and forest green. The small stream we are now fishing flows through a deep cut in the high plains not far below the Alberta border on wide-open tribal land. A friend of ours has given us access to this seldom-fished stretch of water, a couple of miles of lunatic perfection we reach first by highway outside of Browning, a road that diminishes to two-track then finally gives up all pretension of purpose and turns into a chaotic ride across a plowed field of rock and boulders. We park on a cut bank above the water, work our way downstream and start casting the hoppers, always the hoppers for us this time of year.

Rainbow trout race to the surface every time the flies hit the water. As soon as the terrestrial imitations land near a midstream obstruction or along an undercut rocky shelf or above a splashing riffle, the fish tag the bugs. All of them are leapers and all of them are healthy fish. Strong, silvery trout that haven't been bothered in years as our friend laughingly assured us earlier in the day. He finds us amusing and is amazed as he says that we "are allowed loose without adult supervision." Knowing how to go invisible helps, helps a lot.

A flat-out amazing stream dancing through arid, empty land. The only sign of humans is an old wooden house, windows broken out, roof long blown away, sideboards weathered a wind-battered grey. If there was a road that led to a bridge that crossed this stream, which there isn't, and if you looked down into the pure water, you'd say "Too shallow and trout don't swim in this kind of country anyway." But the stream is deeper than it looks. Swift runs over bright gravels look skinny when standing on a grassy bank fifty above. Once in the stream, the flow pushes against our stomachs with chilly friendliness as we work upstream. Blue-green pools are ten-feet deep or more, the streambed hidden in darkness.

Four hours of easy fishing makes us believe we have a grip on what we're doing, but we know better. Unfished, unspoiled, damn good water always makes us feel this way. Put us on a pretentious spring creek and we start crying within thirty minutes. Fifteen-foot, 6x leaders. Size 22 patterns. Skillful presentations. Entomological insights. Educated salmonids. Forget it. Size 6 hoppers and 3x tippet are our speed, especially when coupled with wild, cooperative trout.

Much later in the season we stop in at the Cleveland Bar, an aging wooden joint hiding out in the Bears Paw Mountains. It's Sunday morning. Earlier we fished brush-choked Peoples Creek with tiny dries for little brook trout. Now we are on our way back to the Sun for one last splash before winter shows up. My friend walks into the old, vine-covered place for a quick drink. I stand outside in the breeze, smoking and looking at mountains that appear gentle at first touch, but the more I look the tougher they become. Good country. We could disappear without effort back in here. Raucous laughter ricochets through the screen door and open windows.

"I thought for sure you were from New Hampshire. Live free or die!" roars a deep voice.

"You don't know shit, Tim," this time a feminine one. "Anyone can tell she's from Minnesota. It's in her eyes. Look at them."

I smoke my way through this conversation, riding the wind up a brushy draw, through a grove of aspen and on up to a rocky ridge. Time disappears until my companion exits laughing and shouting over her shoulder "It's in my eyes."

With an inept sense of the appropriate I put on "Low Life" by Donald Bird and we wander off towards the Sun and our campsite several hours away to the west. This time we listen to the music all the way through and I began to think there was at least a small ray of hope for us. And later after pasta with invisible sauce, and grilled vegetables, we sit around the fire watching stars come out and out and out. But we eventually get cold feet and go to sleep.

The wind is insane by the time we crawl out for coffee. Snow, sleet, rain, hail - all of it is coming down, but out of some desperate need to prove to myself and to her that I still am the crazy, take-it-as-it-comes angler of the past, I string the line through the guides and tie on a fat, brown Woolly Bugger. Even 0x tippet is elusive in the cold. I settle for a lame clinch knot. The whole thing probably takes twenty minutes and I look around. She's gone. Where now? I wonder. Looking towards the river for the hell of it and there she is standing in the water up to her hips casting into the teeth of a harsh wind. I can see her laughing and can imagine the sound ringing once again in my ears. Way ahead of me as usual. And now long gone forever. I took care of that.

The hell with "Out To Lunch."

It's high time for Ornette Coleman's "Snowflakes And Sunshine."

And that's that little tune, one that prompted John Wesley, no sarcasm intended, to write this poem called **motion** ...

*... keeping at it all the time*
*with a quick shuffle*
*makes as much sense*
*as other stuff*
*we own today*
*sometimes clarity*
*trips into the movement*
*scary but feels good*
*too bad it is*
*temporary in nature*
*when making do with battery acid*
*juicing through veins*
*passes for living*
*the current jumps starts stops*
*that cannot be the rhythm*
*we were born with*
*not lurching*
*not sneaking*
*wail fearless*
*dance spinning on one foot*
*mad gleam*
*all hell fearless*
*the band is union*
*and will not play long*

# CHAPTER 6
## Island Insanity

### Crazies

*one of a kind, one of us, we are them,*
*rising up northeast of town shoulder next to Sheep*
    *Mountain*
*a small band of outlaw mountains hiding out like many*
    *of us*
*an island range some call them*
*they climb thousands of feet*
*above the high plains*
*but seem happiest when the sky*
*is dead clear blue for dozens and dozens of miles all*
    *around them*
*yet their mad summits are obscured by dark, ragged*
    *sheets of swirling storm clouds*
*tiny creeks run down from the high country*
*eventually becoming streams with wild, native*
    *Yellowstone cutthroat trout in them*
*further down in the wide, open valleys rivers hold*
    *browns, rainbows, brookies, whitefish*
*this is what draws me to these isolated mountains*
*the aloofness, the trout, the strange weather, the lack of*
    *people, the high peaks*
*I'll walk off from old logging roads and catch trout the*
    *length of my index finger*
*and maybe see a grizzly or a wolf that biologists say*
    *aren't here*
*hard to argue with hard headed science, though*
*stands of old Ponderosa survivors rise thick-trunk, red-*
    *bark, banged up from*
*centuries of wind, cold, heat, drought, fire*

on the north end of the lunacy lies the Musselshell and
 prime grassland
to the east is an openness that measures itself in the
 earth's curvature
south past the Interstate and whizzing traffic stretch
 Absaroka and Beartooth
west is the Shields Valley then the straight-up Bridgers
right in the damn middle of all that's right about this place
 stand the Crazies
if only they'll let you really see them on a clear day

**HOW IN THE HELL DID I GET HERE?** – a
question John Wesley has often asked himself whether
sober, drunk, stoned, tired or even feeling on top of his
game. I've fished this stretch of the Shields River many
times, but everything seems madly changed in the most
unnoticeable of ways. I've been here spring, summer
and, finest of all, autumn.

Early October is when large browns lose their
secretive, shadowy behavior. The trout, now driven by
the spawning urge, are roaming the shallow, gravel
runs where the females will build their redds in earnest
in a week or so. In summer they are holding-out way
back in the darkness of brushy, undercut banks. Most
times browns are secretive, loners. Even the chaotic
splash of a suicidal grasshopper a few feet out in the
open water rarely causes them to move. Nymphs,
minnows, smaller trout, any of these that happen to
wander in front of the large predators will be killed
quickly, but otherwise they won't budge. I know. I've
tried launching everything from woolly buggers to
hefty nymphs to saltwater patterns like Deceivers.
Rarely will one of the browns take my offering, one
made with the most honest of intentions. I want to
connect, to feel a wild fish as it runs for cover at the bite
of the hook or walks and crashes along the surface. The

trout's fight for survival makes me feel alive. Perhaps a cruel way to get one's kicks, but I'm a predator, too – fish, birds, mammals of any species – and a darkly spiritual one above all else.

So after taking a half-dozen browns, a small brook trout and a Yellowstone cutthroat, everything is pretty much as I've always remembered it over the years. I notice this as I sit down on a fallen tree trunk along the bank. The stream is low and clear. The streambed sparkles in gem-like colors beneath the gold-copper light of the fall sun. The leaves on willows, birch and cottonwoods are going brilliant yellow, manipulating light in carefree ways. The undergrowth is a mixture of colorful life and death – the buff browns of dying grasses swirled with riffs of crimson and purple from wild berries and rosehips. The freshly-white peaks of the Crazies are visible over the ridge in the east and the Bridgers glow dark-blue, grey and white. Shadows tinted in the same shades creep down the mountain cirques and valleys as the sun moves west. A pair of sandhill cranes clacks away in that dying grass. I see their heads and necks bobbing and lurching as they strut away from me. Strings of geese are moving south with their common cries. Pairs of mallards whistle through the air. Deer silently observe my movements from a distance, as do Angus cattle that pause from their loud munchings to check me out. The last dregs of this year's mayflies bounce above the river's surface. Ahead I see an oval depression of newly cleared stone. The first brown trout spawning bed. One of many that will be dotted along this isolated stretch of water before much longer.

Yeah, all of this seems the same, but just like the end of last season and the one before and so on, everything is different in ways that are visible, but not to the eyes. This valley and everywhere else I travel in

Montana at this time of the year seems to have shifted to a slightly different slice of time than the one I'm buzzing in. There's just enough of this movement to make me feel as though I'm in the middle of the gentlest of earthquakes or passing through a mild moment of dizziness. I feel like I'm in a room where the furniture has been subtly rearranged with such sophistication that I can't notice the changes.

I know I'm crazy. Have been so as long as I can remember. I once had some concern about this to the extent that I used to down large quantities of whiskey to try and feel sane. Didn't work. Drunk is drunk, and hungover is hell growing ever larger as I get older. The changes I'm experiencing aren't associated with being loony. They seem to be more involved with experience and the smallest of advancements in awareness. One would think that an individual as self-absorbed as myself would see any growth in perception as enormous, but it doesn't work that way. And I've noticed all of this for years in a number of places. Fishing's to blame. Hanging out in undisturbed nowhere is at fault. Casting to trout or bass or pike is strong stuff, much stronger than the whiskey I mentioned. The power has little to do with landing a large trout, though, like sex, following fly fishing to its commonly accepted conclusion is of brief satisfaction, which differs from killing of any kind with its permanent lust, rush, regret, remorse.

I first drifted through this mild oddity in vision a dozen years ago down at Tongue River country, the home of my heart. The coulees, eroding rock, native grasses, turkeys, coyotes and the vast aloneness are sensible to me. One October I'd shot a pair of sharptail grouse on a flat just off the red-dust two-track that winds to a dry camp I have near a stand of old Ponderosa. There were lots of the birds feeding on fat crickets. When they took wing at my approach, their flight was labored. The shooting straightforward. Next I drove to a pond that used to hold rainbows, still does in a non-fishing way. An hour of relaxed casting netted me several trout. I killed one to go with my grouse-baked potato-roasted-onion dinner. As I was cleaning this fish I felt as though the landscape slipped sideways. I put the rainbow in the cooler on ice, opened a Pabst, lit a smoke and looked around. The land was silent. Nothing but yellow sunlight shifting towards orange moving over the country dragging purple shadows with it. This was as alone as I'd ever felt. Like the only person on the planet. In some ways I was terrified. Then giving in to the unnamed but obviously deep fear, a sense of power ripped through me. The rush faded. I have no concept of what is meant by serenity, but I felt at peace for the first time in I don't know how many damn years. What had I done to earn this respite from the day-to-day anxiety? Well, I'd walked a windy flat, killed a couple of birds and then fished for some trout. Nothing more or less. Not one for examining my psychological navel like way too many others. I finished my beer and moved on.

Since that little country ditty there have been many other moments of oh-so-modest revelation. Fishing the Yellowstone here in Livingston with a longtime friend. Hooking a brown and then slipping on a rock, falling in and gaily floating downstream with the angry fish pulling on my line as I tried to keep the rod above water and avoid drowning. I lost the fish, but saved my life. I remember the sound of my companion laughing from his vantage point on a high cut bank and his yelling "Gill, I can't understand why Orvis won't send you any more stuff. You're fly fishing's poster child." And then that slight lateral shift of reality, life, whatever, materialized. A touch of fear, aloneness (not loneliness, that's something else) and then happy calm. I doubt I would have felt this way at a sports bar or a concert or a restaurant.

I've never been much for fishing with guides or doing the in thing like traveling to the latest hot river or lodge. I'm a true loner, like the browns, and simpler is better. It avoids confusion and eventual torment. I don't need, certainly don't want, some over-charging Bozo dressed to the nines in the latest fly fishing on-the-stream fashion statement telling me where to cast, how to cast, how to play a fish or let me know by a serious of orchestrated smirks, shrugs, frowns and snide comments what a half-assed angler and probably, human being, I am. Fishing alone or with one or at most two good friends is how fly fishing, bird hunting, any outdoor avocation, was shown to me. Catching fish - yes, that's nice. Killing a few chukar – not bad either. Owning quality gear that makes all of this easier and more enjoyable – nothing wrong here. But that's not really the point. Those who have patiently guided me along a life that centers on good country have all said in their own curious ways, "That's cool that you made that cast that caught that fish, but that's not what's important. What counts, kid, is that river you're standing in. Those mountains over there. That blood-red prairie we crossed at sunrise - how all of it makes you feel. That's the wild game you're really after."

And I finally grasped the natural concept. Basically it's brain-dead simple. Lose the ego. Submit to the land. Connect with the feral buzz, then recognize my insignificant yet worthwhile place in the untamed, unfathomable scheme of things. None of the good stuff is related to fancy clothing, pricey fly rods or $5,000-a-week lodge gigs. Get wet and a little muddy. Then feel good enough to slide along in a strange dance for no good reason.

The light of October is special. It glows with an amber influence. I look up from my tree-trunk seat and spot a brown holding in a soft run about forty feet upstream. Only its fins and slight flicks of its tail reveal motion. Slowly I work out line to cover the distance, make the cast and start the retrieve. The fish hits the pattern with its head once, then again. It circles back and slams the streamer. The white of its mouth flashes. This fish thrashes across the surface, tires quickly and comes easily to me as I kneel in a few inches of water. Reds, browns, blacks, pale greens and bronze flanks. The lower jaw is formed into a hook or a kype. A male. I twist the hook free and watch as the trout swims slowly across stream to a deep hole beneath the tangled roots of an old cottonwood. And my fragile, lunatic world shifts casually out of kilter. I'm a bit afraid, then serene again, then laughing. "Completely nuts, Gill," I say out loud to no one; and feel good about it all, good enough to write this thing called **upstream all the way** ...

*starts in an inland sea*
*ends in a small creek*
*where grizzlies hang out*
*bad enough*
*fighting the ones*
*wanting to rip you*
*out of the water*
*dodging deadfalls*
*boulders, gravel slides*
*current shows the way*
*farther up*
*less water to fight*
*familiar flow calls*
*smaller now*
*drive stronger*

*rock recognized color*
*forest shade*
*converting rhythm*
*way back up here*
*thin riffles*
*small pools*
*both times*
*the same place*

... Later that night when bourbon and internal darkness that was anything but emptiness and not really form overtook him because he was tired, a bit worn out from the road, as he sat around a very late night fire he wrote another one about not feeling so good ...

**inside angles**

*not much known*
*about the tallest*
*and maybe oldest of them*
*quiet, staredown eyes,*
*usually dead still*
*motionless,*
*even by the other four*
*despite the thousands*
*of down time*
*dead end hours*
*burned*
*while standing*
*slouching, shifting*
*on their corner*
*in front of Mickey's Liquors*
*Dubois Pawn – Payroll Checks Cashed Here -*
*The Turtle Tap*
*The Mint*
*all nearby*

*he keeps to himself*
*is called Ed*
*maybe fifty-five*
*maybe thirty*
*who the hell knows*
*the years make liars*
*of all of us*
*allow persona shifts*
*largely undetectable*
*even by stone wolves*

*spinning around*
*drive me nuts*
*like a bad advertising jingle*
*of John Dean's "this point in time" doublespeak*
*always the damn images*
*of what might have been*
*an easy life in the mountains*
*away from the bs*
*fishing for cutthroat*
*working the ridges for spruce and blues*
*playing tag with grizzlies*
*walking with elk, moose*
*invisible murders took it away*
*all that's lost now*
*and the loss*
*won't leave me in peace*
*won't give me a break*
*I killed her*
*she had it coming and*
*she knew it*
*betrayed my trust and love*
*with lust, drank me down*
*like cold beer on a*
*smoking July afternoon*
*the bottle dripping*

*icy condensation*
*screwed my best friend*
*was doing this*
*when I walked in*
*from that long day*
*fixing fence*
*beneath a bastard sun*
*peaks of eastern Glacier*
*flashing white, purple*
*down east in the clouds*
*Sweet Grass Hills glowing west*
*and they both laughed*
*when they saw that I saw*
*was shocked, wounded*
*so I went to the truck*
*reached under the seat*
*grabbed the .357*
*shot him in the knees, the gut*
*her between the eyes*
*loud crashes, no sound*
*smell of gunpowder ignited*
*haze of blue smoke*
*what a mess*
*blood, bone and brains*
*splattered all over the bed*
*windows, walls, rug*
*dogs scared as hell*
*ran away*
*someone down the road heard*
*called the cops*
*remember running through the aspens*
*limbs and leaves smelling green*
*slapping my face and hands*
*in the starlight dark*
*down to the hi-line tracks*
*timed my jump into a*

*Great Northern boxcar*
*froze my ass off*
*when it crested the divide*
*Marias Pass*
*cars creaking and lurching*
*over uneven rails*
*always remember the smell*
*of diesel exhaust*
*from those five Dash 9's*
*powering up the mountains*
*heard avalanches crashing,*
*whispering loud death*
*as tons of snow, ice, rock*
*sluiced over the wooden sheds*
*skipped in Havre*
*at the depot*
*scored a pint of Beam*
*at the liquor store*
*across the street*
*hitched a ride on US 2*
*with a trucker*
*then another down 16 to Sidney*
*and made it all the way to here*
*which is nowhere*
*I'd ever heard of*
*a place that maybe doesn't exist*
*out on the high plains*
*where sometimes I think*
*that my madness*
*can see clearly*
*from sea to shining sea*
*thank any God for these four*
*they don't ask*
*and I don't tell*
*we drink away the days*
*all of this hurts hard*

*but there's a little peace*
*now and then*
*enough so we can*
*catch our breath*
*and they're friends*
*trust like no other*
*we've got nothing else*

*and really none of them*
*are hip to all that much*
*about any of our past lives*
*doesn't matter, who cares*
*all of it is dead and gone*
*worthless, blown away*
*like that gunsmoke*
*hanging out on the corner*
*where life is cheap*
*and getting high*
*drunk, stoned*
*is more a useful habit*
*that adds only a little*
*to the river light*
*they ride each day*
*maybe the one the other four*
*know so little about*
*was a big deal*
*back when*
*back where*
*none of them are interested*
*passing round the pint of Kessler's*
*smoking stale Chesterfields*
*taking it all in*
*as nothing at all*
*keeps on happening*

# CHAPTER 7

## A Lack of Exercise

**DAMN HOT. LATE APRIL. LOW NINETIES.** I'm too old and out of shape to be doing this John Wesley," he thinks. He'd been wandering around the red sand flat a 1,000 feet below the South Rim of the Canyon during the morning then struggled back up the trail in the growing heat. Heading down the trail at dawn the sunrise was a good one. Every shade of red, yellow, orange and blue he could image flashed across thin reefs of clouds, the light running hot then fading as it moved along the clouds. At the edge of the plateau I looked down hundreds of feet, down through the next serious cut in the rock that spans millions of years of linear time, down into a dry wash of scrub and jumbled boulders. He stared into that for a long time and watched as dark purple shadows slid across the ground and finally vanished beneath the climbing sun.

Eventually he turned back and started the short, steep climb to my camp. The sun wasn't cutting me any breaks as he walked the last few hundred yards to a stock tank where he'd parked my old Suburban beneath some pines. Gill's feet kicked up puffs of grey- and ochre-colored dust. I kicked a few desiccated pine cones ahead of him. This place was only a few hours away from the tourista madness of Bright Angel Lodge, but no one ever came here. Too far away. No guided pack trips. No curio shops. No restaurants. And the big tour buses from LA and Vegas would high-center before they lurched too far into this isolated country. The two-track leading in soon degenerates into a free-form exercise in dodge-the-rocks, watch out for the jackrabbits. The stock tank where I set up camp was full of cool, clean water that was replenished by the efforts of an old, rusting windmill. A luxury in this parched land. All the water he would ever need and no cattle. Never had seen one in all the times he'd been here. Not an Angus or a Hereford or, sadly, a longhorn. Loved those Spanish-blooded beasts. At the tank John Wesley reached down through the water pulled a cooler from the water and fished around for a can of Pabst buried in the ice. He took a long pull of the beer and then another before looking around.

The sky was light blue burning to white-silver as the sun hammered away. Nothing moved. No wind. No sound. Gill was alone. The intense light of midday turned the small pines a dusty green and the soil simmered, waves of radiating heat distorting the air making spectral images of the landscape. Well above a small rise not so far away, a pair of vultures circled, enormous dihedral wings curled slightly to take advantage of the thermals. The birds rose higher and higher slicing the sky. Black ghosts against the sharp horizon. He looked away from them and down at my sweat-soaked shirt. His jeans and tennis shoes were covered with the colorful dust from down below.

A fantastic place. The kind of land the man could disappear in forever.

He didn't really work anymore. He'd Jim Beamed his way out of a crappy job with a small Mickey Mouse daily up north in Montana, but money wasn't an issue. Every time he considered this financial blessing, Blood, Sweat and Tears' cover of "God Bless the Child" ran through his head. David Clayton Thomas deep, rich voice singing about rich relations and such. Yeah they gave him money to stay lost, way out of sight. He'd blown a "career," and was considered an embarrassment to his clan. Get lost sport. Stay out of sight. Every month enough family cash found its way into Gill's account to allow him to wander the high, dry country of Utah, Nevada, New Mexico and the Kaibab Plateau here in Arizona. He still wrote a story every so often for one of the fly fishing magazines, but that was because he was born a writer, and even if he didn't write John Wesley was always looking at things the way real writers do. Like an x-ray technician on acid. Always seeing things most others didn't, like that blue light flickering across the tops of the trees and shooting electric connections to a pile of crazy rocks not so far away on that rise where the vultures flew. And on and on.

No job. Not too many worries. He'd given up on being a productive member of society a bunch of mistakes ago. Enjoyed the hell out of the people he met on the road. Like the guy at the Exxon yesterday who poured in 40 gallons of Premium Plus for about $600. Maybe not quite that much. Took so long the pair killed off a pack of smokes and a six-pack in the process. He was a Cubs fan and liked to fish so it was easy time. Then Gill drove on down an empty, sunset highway like he'd never been here before and wasn't really here now. A crazy life, but, then, all of it seemed a little nuts when he covered the cops up in Shelby for another little newspaper. The constant wind driving all of us over the edge. Ranchers found just driving their Massey Fergusons in endless circles out in wheat fields the size of New Hampshire, or people betting who could eat the most pickled pigs feet in five minutes at The Mint Bar. And he was supposed to write about this. Yeah, whiskey has its moments, but there were a few too many up that way. He finally couldn't take it anymore and the managing editor couldn't either. That was some years back and now he was here.

Over on the ridge the vultures were gliding low across the rise, banking sharply and coming in lower over a spot near a lone juniper. He finished his beer, secured another and went off to see what the big deal was.

What seemed a 100 yards was more like a half mile. The clarity of the natural situation here had tricked me, but John Wesley got there. The birds rose up at his approach, the air moving across their feathers sounding like gentle wind slipping through the trees. At first he couldn't see anything because of the intense light. Then he spotted the body not far from the juniper. Gill had seen his share of corpses doing the police reporting deal and during living in general, so this one wasn't something new. And whoever this person had once been, had been here for some time. The dry climate, the heat, the wind and, no doubt, scavengers had cleaned things up. Mainly bones and some ragged, torn clothes. Jeans, shirt, tennis shoes, and a bunch of beer cans scattered around. Schmidt. Used to drink Schmidt, but that was a few years back. Bitter tasting after a couple of cans. Some brown hair still clung to the skull. Beneath one hand was a book. The cover bleached and when he pulled it from beneath the bones the pages crumbled. He could barely make out the title. ***Blood Sport***. A little-known classic by Robert F. Jones. Gill had had a few drinks with the guy once in Casper and he was alright. A little crazy, a touch surly and a hell of a storyteller. They got along for those few hours at least. Never seen him since. Whoever this body had once been ... well, hell, he could have been John Wesley. Dying out on the high flats of the southwest full of cheap beer and Bob Jones. He could see it. There'd most likely be a pint of Beam in there somewhere, though if he was involved.

Gill thought about reporting the body to the police when he returned to town somewhere, but decided not to. Dead is dead, and he did not want to interrupt the important course of his life by dealing with the authorities.

He turned away and started back to the stock tank. Half-way there an image of the dead man, perfectly formed but without substance, liquid clear, zipped through him like his body went through Gill's in an instant with the slightest ripple of feeling, like a very mild shock. Odd he thought and aimed for the cooler.

Setting a cold beer on a low, weathered wooden shed that protected the water output for the tank, taking off his clothes and stepping over the edge of the galvanized aluminum tank, managing to catch his foot on the edge and splash head-first into water that was maybe 60 degrees. Damn near stopped his heart. He stands up in a chaotic spray and lets the sun dry him while working on the Pabst. Naked to the world.

Then the vultures blasted in at tree top level moving at a good clip. They dipped towards me. He ducks and can feel the rush of hot air rushing across their two-toned black wings as they roared overhead. The pair dips down lower, maybe six feet above the ground, before soaring up the rise where the body lay. He reaches over the edge for another beer. When John Wesley turns back they were gone and he's back in the past tense.

The afternoon was hotter now, the air dead still. Cooking. Lifeless.

He wondered what he'd be doing tomorrow.

~ ~ ~

Gill rolled under a sagging, rusting strand of barbed-wire fence. As he did so a brief story he'd written a long time ago for Big Sky Journal, back before it became Big Sky Yuppy Spawn Maunderings, wandered into the front of his brain ...

... My difficulties with fences began some years ago, a delicate transmutation arising from problems I had and still have with gates. Either my hands get scratched from trying to latch the ragged compilations of weathered tree limbs and barbed wire that block passage to some exotic fishing water or I pinch my fingers in the workings of the newer hook-type mechanism or I become inextricably tangled in the wire while crossing through. And with the certainty of an eastern-horizon sunrise, I find myself on the wrong sides of these gates after closing them. Coming or going, it doesn't matter. The Suburban is always beyond the gate waiting for me to figure things out.

When I turned fifty crossing fences turned into a struggle. I'm in fairly good shape, not too much overweight, and manage to totter around with a modest degree of authority, but now I cannot get over, under or through a fence, particularly barbed wire ones, without some sort of mishap. All of the shirts I wear fishing or bird hunting are torn along the shoulders and back. My sweaters have loops pulled from their tight knitting large enough to hold ice axes, and my waders leak, doing little more now than visually announce that I'm about to chase some fish.

One time along the Shields River I became entangled while stooping and grunting through some wire that silently guarded a delightful stretch of prime water. Frustrated - I could hear trout splashing after caddis less than 30 feet away- I jerked free only to have the tip guide of my fly rod hook on a rusty barb. Jerking the rod sharply I lost my footing, the rod separating at mid section. I slid to the bottom of the embankment with line humming off the reel as though I'd hooked a five-pound brown. Nothing serious came of this calamity. I lost a few minutes of my life during regrouping. The tip guide was bent into a narrow oval and my torn shirt was now more torn. I was dusty and bedraggled, but that's how I wind up looking after fishing anyway. I went on to have a pleasant day catching a few browns, but that incident was the beginning of my firm dislike for fences and an beginning of an awareness concerning our obsession with closing land in, delineating, and not so tacitly stating that, a given piece of property that is owned is now longer a part of what's left of free range in the West.

We're all obsessed with possession. Relationships between the sexes are often defined by the scars of these emotional turf wars. That's to be expected. We're a flawed species. And purchasing a piece of land is overt possession, but controlling this land is absurd. Yeah, I understand that if someone pays the bucks they can do what they want with the acreage. Cattle must be managed. And riffraff such as myself needs to be kept at bay. A dwindling few ranchers still allow access to their land if a person politely asks and remembers to thank them with a Christmas bottle of rye whiskey or such. But the whole ownership thing is out of control on the high plains. Orange spray-painted fence posts by the millions, "Keep Out" signs swaying in the wind and "No hunting or fishing. No trespassing" warnings. How a person can do the former two without committing the latter is a mystery. This variation seems a case of restating the obvious. If you can't pass, you logically can't fish or hunt.

And I love the entrances to many of the newer ranches or ranchettes, the ones marked by a pair of enormous Ponderosa pine trunks topped by an equally large trunk across the top. And dangling below the top brace in clear examples of human hauteur are signs that dance to the tune of "Smith's Ponderosa" or "Knodle's Wild West Retreat" or, my personal favorite, "Wall Street Retreat." Thankfully the plains Indians never adopted this insecure form of territorialism.

Visions of "Plenty Coups' Palace" or "Dull Knife's Estancia" come shakily to mind.

All of this makes sense to me. Let's all hem in the land and its spirit with miles of barbed wire and then announce to the world who exactly is responsible for this self-absorbed mayhem. Like we own the good country in the long term. Recent wildfires in Montana and now California say otherwise, as do drought, earthquake and the inevitable ice age. I've never been a wannabe Indian. Not my style, and quite sensibly on the tribes' part, they don't want me, but whatever happened to respecting the land that can never be truly owned? What about honoring and submitting to the long-running buzz that is the electric spirit of the West?

Sure fencing one's property ensures at least the illusion of privacy and security. We can all drive down our private, dusty lanes, sit on the front porch and arrogantly say while sipping some expensive single malt, "I've got mine. You can't have it. I'm really living now." The mentality that made us great hideously guts the essence of open space.

Up until a few years ago I couldn't imagine what Montana or the Dakotas would have been like 150 years ago. A land of no fences, few people and a vastness filled with wild animals that rivaled Africa's now ravaged Serengeti. For the past several years I've been drifting up to the far north of the Yukon and Northwest Territories with increasing frequency while researching a book. When I first drove through the hundreds of miles of uncut boreal forest and crossed rivers like the Mackenzie that are more than a mile wide and 40 feet deep, when I saw thousands of woodland bison grazing by the dirt roads that are called highways up there, I was blown away. To finally experience such an immense wealth of wilderness, an area many times the size of Montana, with so few signs of people was staggering. To catch countless grayling of several pounds from one small stretch of river was stunning. One day last June as I cruised up to the First Nations Dene De Cho settlement of Pedzah Ki, I watched the Mackenzie flow, not flow but power, its way north to above the Arctic Circle and finally into the Beaufort Sea. The Canyon Range, then the Mackenzie Range, then other mountains rolled away to the west for hundreds of miles. Moose ghosted through stands of dwarf birch. Black bears were all over the place feeding on the green, rich grasses of a short, intense summer. Through binoculars I sighted grizzlies wandering the slopes of the McConnell Range. Fifty miles to the south, Nahanni Butte shimmered silvery blue. For days I saw only a few settlements of maybe 100 people each. No phone or electric lines. No fences. The difference in the energy, in the feel, of this land was palpable. The countryside sizzled and seemed to flicker with a light that is not seen by the eyes. This must have been what the Big Sky felt like a couple of centuries past. Montana is home in my heart, but the North in its, for now, untamed radiance owns my soul.

Experiencing all of this up north made me see that we don't improve things for ourselves or, more importantly, for the good country when we attempt to stamp our designs of control on the landscape. Instead we cut out the heart of the place and in the process slice away chunks of ourselves. In a few years my children will be off to college and I'm going to move out of Livingston and back into the empty, open spaces. I'd like to believe that I'll tear down all of the fences on whatever place I find, but knowing myself, I doubt it. I want my piece of paradise just like anyone else.

Last October while returning from another day fishing on the Shields I crossed several fences on the way back to the Suburban. Angus cattle were casually grazing on the last of the year's good grass. As is normal these days, I fought with a fence near the highway. When I finally passed through I looked up and saw a lone cow standing on the roadside of the fence. Cattle do this. They always want what they see on the other side, then decide that they really need to return to their original side of the obstruction. The animal was pushing against the barbed wire trying to rejoin its herd. The cow bawled in its frustration. A large gash ran along its flank. Blood from the wound glistened in the sunlight. I turned away, unlocked the back doors of the rig and started to put away my gear. I looked down at my right hand. A long scratch ran from the base of the little finger to the wrist. There was a good deal of blood that, too, glistened in the light.

Pondering all of this – the lunacy of walking beneath a hot sun at the Grand Canyon or participating in arduous combat with fences of various lineage got me to realizing that so much of what I do makes absolutely no sense or on a good day, very little. I used to worry this over in my mind sometimes. Not any more. I do what I do and the hell with figuring out the intrinsic meaning or value of my actions.

### soft and lazy – inspired by Natalie Merchant

*their minds are soft and lazy*
*she sang with a bunch of maniacs*
*so many years ago*
*and like most other stuff she writes*
*she nailed this one on its dull head*
*but she's kinder than I*
*and suggests giving them what they want*
*they won't remember*
*where I would get in their heads*
*and insist that they be held*
*accountable for their*

*venalities, dishonesties,*
*their thoughtless behaviors*
*never give an inch on this one*
*but that's why she is who she is*
*and so many of us care for*
*her energetic, hopeful ideals*
*and I'm wandering the*
*high plains screaming*
*at an empty sky*

# CHAPTER 8

## Don't Forget to Turn Out the Lights

**JOHN WESLEY LOVED THE ARCTIC**. The Northwest Territories. The Yukon. The sub arctic wilderness of northern British Columbia and the boreal forest that stretched for hundreds of miles in all directions beginning down in northern Alberta around the dive, dusty, windswept town of High Level. The first time he tried to reach for the Arctic Circle along the Dempster Highway in the Yukon he met with a bit of a disruption. He laughs whenever he thinks of this misadventure that ended better than it might have or even should have considering much of his disruptive karma.

~ ~ ~

The remains of my suburban are down in the bottom of Engineer Creek gulch. The rig is lying upside-down, smashed, flattened, ruined. I am sitting in the middle of the greasy-turning-to-ice mess of a road, my face bloodied, right wrist sprained, jeans torn from the ragged escape. A storm is wailing down from the southern slopes of the moon-like Richardson Mountains, ice-hard snow slamming into the ground and ripping across the grey-brown-drab green countryside in a quality Yukon whiteout. The light is a ghostly (ghastly?) silvery blue in the dimming light of an early October afternoon. For several days I'd been way back in this isolated bit of nowhere camping by myself along a small stream that was loaded with 12-inch grayling. I caught dozens of them, keeping a few each evening for dinner. By now the grizzlies and black bears were either denned up or leaning in the direction, so I wasn't concerned about an ursine raid on my camp.

Cautious in a clean camp way, but not worried. Aside from the blued-gun-metal finish fish and a moose wandering the swampy margins of the creek here and there, most of the wildlife seemed to be long gone. I heard a few random groups of ducks and Canada geese beating their wings frantically as they headed south. Around noon today from a vantage point on the crest of a rock ridge over 1,500 feet above camp I saw a ragged, boiling line of spinning storm clouds beating down from the north. The weather had been crisp, autumn perfect. I'd even managed to catch a few grayling in several calm runs of the Olgilvie, a river that for some reason had been difficult for me to fish successfully in past years. The river was about a mile down a wide, treeless valley where rounded, barefaced mountains rose up on both sides finally joining in a curving crest several miles from the road. I followed a game trail both up to my camp as it worked through tundra now past its peak autumn colors and showing soft tan, brown and ochre. And I'd walk further down along the creek to where it joined with the Olgilvie after rushing through a narrow band of timber and brush. The two waters formed a large, slowing circling pool that held the fish, often just along the spiral foam edges. Drifting a nymph in this turned a number of 15-17 inch grayling. Then I'd relax after dinner around late-night fires, as I puffed on Cuban cigars and what not. Well after dark when the stars and the aurora made their appearances the mournful howls of wolves along the mountain crests would float down to camp. The wild calls mixed with everything else in this great valley. I'd had a peaceful time up to the point of winter's mad approach.

I raced back down the mountain. Throwing everything into the back of the Suburban, I thought I could beat the front if I managed to slip through this

300-foot slippery dip in the Dempster Highway that eventually returned to relatively decent road, relatively speaking, that heads to the Klondike Highway and Dawson City about 200 miles away. A cabin at Klondike Kate's, a long, hot shower, some grilled salmon and pasta at the restaurant next door, some bourbon and then a peaceful night reading of Exley's *Pages From a Cold Island* were calling. I was wrong. I didn't make it. Even creeping along in four-wheel-drive the rig begin to slip gathering speed as soon it pointed its nose over the rise that gave way to a steep grade. I had no control over the situation. In seconds the machine decided to see what was over the abrupt edge. I pushed open the door and rolled out, bouncing in the slop like a paint can tossed from the window of a fast-moving 1964 Chevy Impala. While sliding along doing my own dysfunctional two-step I could hear sounds of metal crunching and tearing and glass shattering. All I remember saying was "Oh shit!" as the car disappeared from sight. I should have stayed put at my camp and waited out the snow, but Edgar Allen Poe's *The Imp of the Perverse* got the better of me and I made a moron's decision. I've made many of these over the years. This one ranks right up there in the top five.

Now what? I step to the edge of the drop-off and look below. I sit down on my ass and began to work my way down to the bottom of the draw. The bank is loose gravel, mud, rocks, fir trees tilting at precarious angles in the thin soil, roots exposed. There is food, a tent and some matches down there. Eventually this blizzard will let up, though it is howling now through the dead ground cover, brush and dormant trees. Some trucker hauling fuel or food farther up the road above the Arctic Circle to Inuvik will notice the wreck on his way up the road tomorrow or the next day.

Engineer Creek flows dirty orange from the

dissolved mineral content and my Suburban is tan and brown. Maybe the wreck won't be as easy to spot as I just thought. What the hell? Someone will eventually spot the mess and me. In time I'd have another foolish story to tell. And at least the Suburban hadn't exploded in a fireball of over-priced gas. As the weather continues to fall apart by the minute, I can just make out the rig's dark, battered shape. Eventually I reach the wreck, very cold, soaked and frozen. The need to start a fire is obvious. There is plenty of wood in the form of gnarled limbs and sticks lying along the sides of the narrow streambed and now being covered in snow.

My waxed cotton coat and some shooting gloves are hanging out the remains of the passenger side window opening. A wool hat is in one of the coat's pockets. Everything else I need is wedged in the pancaked wreck. I'd attend to the tent and sleeping bag later, but first a fire and some heat. I always carry a box of Ohio Blue Tip matches in one of the coat's many pockets. I clear a spot in the snow in the lee of a boulder, make a fire ring from nearby rocks, lay in a pile of twigs and sticks. I'm beginning to ease off the adrenalin rush of the motorized mayhem. The thought of freezing to death out here flashes briefly then slips away with the swirling wind. I begin to think of family and friends as I prepare to strike the first match.

The flame is bright in the gloom and I imagine that I see my mother sitting in front of the fireplace at her home in Whitefish sipping her customary evening Old Fashion. She turns to me in the flickering light of the match and says, "I always told you to get a cell phone. You never know when something like this will happen and now it has. I hope you weren't drinking when this happened." I hadn't been, though based on past exploits this was a reasonable inquiry. Mom has always been on my side, right there with me through all of the chaos I manage to stagger into, but I find it odd that all of this was taking place within the bright confines of a match flame flickering in my cupped hands. "Call me when you get home," and she turns to the fire, sips her drink and the match goes out. Nice thought about the cell phone, except that I'm way out of range this far up the Dempster.

I find a couple of yellow receipts from the Livingston, Montana Napa Auto Parts store in my pocket – brake pads and a headlight – and work them beneath the twigs. I strike a Blue Tip and it fizzles, smokes and dies. I rip another along the side of the box and it catches. Shoving it next to the paper, hunching over to protect it from the wind with my body, the beginnings of fire curls up to the wood. In the light this time I see a woman I'd known briefly some years ago. She was a good one, but not for me and I never felt any pull towards her or profound romantic attraction. She was interesting in a self-absorbed way and back then that killed some time for me and that was enough. I think to myself 'Gill, you're truly nuts this time around.' But there she is, well-tanned, short brown hair, sitting in a chaise lounge on the front porch of her home along the Bitterroot River near Darby. I can see the thick green grass of her front yard, the crabapple trees and across the gravel road a farmer working a hayfield in the last of the day's sunlight. Her name is Ann Marie and she says quite clearly, her voice sounding like there is no storm raging around me at all, "You know John, if you weren't such an outspoken loner you'd have more friends. As it is now, you either scare the hell out of us or piss us off with your hardcore pronouncements. Ease up on us, would you? And do yourself a favor and cut yourself some slack," and she lights a cigarette with a silver Zippo lighter before concluding with "And lay off the damned booze. You turn into a babbling idiot, repeating yourself over and over. Better yet, just go away for good and leave us in peace," and Ann Marie draws on her Marlboro before blowing out a thick blue cloud of smoke. A puff of icy wind snuffs out the match and the paper. Well, perhaps this charming event will make me "just go away for good." That would be too bad. Ann Marie's a good woman, though her Sicilian blood makes her a bit impatient and hot tempered at times. Has a bit of money, too. One must consider these things, especially with a writer's thin income. I did and said "Not for this kid." I like running my own show, even a destitute one. After all broke is broke. Still, I know that she's still alive and I keep her in the back of my mind for a stormy day.

Nuts or not, I don't need this. I need a fire and then a few drinks to make me an "idiot." Right now I'm a cold, wet idiot. I'd prefer being a warm, drying out idiot. I get up, already stiff from the wreck and the lovely weather and lurch over to the Suburban to see if I can find some more paper. I manage to pull pieces of a reasonably dry grocery bag out from beneath the twisted back seat. I return to my pile of sticks that is somewhat sheltered by the boulder dropped off in this location thousands of years ago by an enormous blast of spring runoff. I pull the box of matches from my coat and try again. Man, just give me some serious flame and none of this concerned advice silliness, though I am curious to see who will show up next.

The match sizzles and bursts into flame, the paper ignites and small sticks began to pop and crackle. I'm home or rather, because of the madness of the wavering flames, I'm sitting on the front steps of my old friend Myerson's home. He is rubbing the ears of his yellow lab Bart or maybe it's Jake. I often confuse the two. He turns to me and starts to say something, and I say once again with original brilliance "Oh shit!!"

"Don't interrupt me, damnit," Myerson said. "We've been friends for a long time. Been through hell and back more than once," and he reaches down for a stick that he tosses in some tall grass. Jake leaps to the chase. "You always run along the precipice of things looking for trouble. Your life isn't some twisted Nabokov novel like *Ada* or *Laughter in the Dark*. And I sure as hell hope isn't *Lolita*. Ease up on yourself. Relax a little. I'd suggest finding a good woman, but we both damn well know how that would turn out. So, get the damn fire going and don't pay any attention to what Ann Marie just said. Make yourself a stiff drink and ride out the night. We've got those browns on the Marias to play with next fall." I start to say something, but a wicked downdraft of frigid air packed with snow mashes my fire into nothing. I smell damp smoke.

Even while I am courting hypothermia, I realize that I am having an episode of sorts. One that is odd even in my arcane experiences. Perhaps I really am nuts or, at least, making a game effort to go in that direction. I've always seen and heard things that either people didn't or wouldn't admit to experiencing or didn't want to believe existed. But with a certain amount of effort I've managed to keep the trip between the white lines to the extent that I've never been locked up in the state mental asylum at Warm Springs. I'm saving that one for when the going really turns rough, like say when I finally make the money I feel I so richly deserve and become the intolerable bastard so many people already think I am. Then I'll need a white room, quality meds and lots of solitude of an institutional variety.

"Screw it," I say and return to getting the fire going.

I strike a lot of matches and hear from a lot of people during the next thirty minutes, but the gods eventually take pity on me and the wood finally burns. I build the sucker up into a blaze by diligently adding stick upon larger stick. Maybe the crash landing on the road up above has knocked me crazier than normal. Maybe I am having a brief interlude with mortality. Whatever. In the coals that glow in the darkness of early night I see everything that is the North Country for me – my friends, the freedom of isolation and the peaceful side of this vast, lonesome and unbelievably powerful land. I begin to warm up and think of getting some more wood and making at least the illusion of shelter with my tent and sleeping bag. The whiteout has transmogrified into a straightforward snowfall. The wind is all but dead and large flakes drift down, many of them hissing before turning to vapor above fire.

From down in this drainage about 200 feet below the Dempster Highway there are no signs of the modern world other than the remains of my rig, which admittedly are substantial. Watching the flames, looking at the tent and the gear I've arranged into a cooking area near the fire circle, I imagine that I'm actually here in a time period 100 years in the past. The Suburban is covered in snow. I visualize it as a large boulder. A few hundred yards downstream of where I'm standing I see the Olgilvie River running wide and pewter along its streambed of stone and silent conifers. The water drifts in and out of view depending on the intensity of the falling snow. The only sounds are the creek slipping down to the river, the cracklings of the fire and the sounds of my breathing. I know that the road is only a couple of minutes away, but I feel completely isolated from the rest of the world. My existence is centered in this concentrated niche of wilderness. Whether I'm ever found or not means nothing to me at this point. I'm already dead or maybe finally alive in the most basic of ways. The difference between these two states no longer exists for me. I place a couple of large pieces of wood across the orange coals that shimmer in waves of heat.

A flicker of movement out at the edges of vision catches my attention. Ann Marie taught me to never look these appearances straight on. Rather, let them fully materialize if that's their intent. This takes practice and will power. Slowly the image becomes concrete and moves slowly into view. An enormous grey wolf. The fur along its back, at the edges of its ears and along its muzzle are shaded towards charcoal. The eyes are black but glow with the light of a being totally alive. We stare at each other through the snow and the growing darkness for I don't know how long. A limb makes a loud snap as it burns through in the fire. My attention is diverted. When I look back the wolf is gone. I walk over to where the animal stood. There are four foot prints where he was. None to mark his coming or going. What can I say? Nothing, so I laugh and return to my fire.

I decide that I'd had enough conversation and most likely one vision too many for this evening. I walk over to the wreck, my boots pushing through a half-foot of Yukon snow, in search of a bottle of whiskey to build that stiff drink Myerson suggested.

~ ~ ~

When I finally had a wrecker right my rig and tow it back down the road to Dawson City for about a thousand bucks- American which is now about 1.4 times Canadian, I had to wait a couple of weeks for repairs to be completed. I killed time in my old cabin at Klondike Kate's and in the restaurant and bar (mostly here) of the establishment. I wrote the above account and a number of poems about the Far North. John Wesley liked this best of all.

### Arctic Aurora

*In a world gone mediocre*
*with television, sound bite blitz*
*and hack work politicians*
*gated golfing communities*
*people making too much money*
*doing absolutely nothing*
*of any value that I can see*
*insane wars, mad policy*
*strip mines, clearcuts, dam*
*murdered romances*
*with all this crap*
*look to the northern sky*
*watch the spiritual ghost dance*
*as unearthly colors*
*of radioactive elegance*
*shade, whisper, cavort*
*peach, azure, vermilion, emerald*
*shadowy luminescence*
*weaving within a backdrop*
*of universal objects*
*alchemy made real*
*as we gain visions*
*from lines of sight*
*zeroing in on prey*
*through a rifle scope*

# CHAPTER 9

### Fade to Black

THE DAMN LIGHT KEPT SWITICHING from green to yellow to red to green to yellow to red for maybe a thousand times now. John Wesley was into the pattern, the three-step dance while lying in the middle of the intersection with the warm rain falling on his face that felt too good for him to move. Cars swerved and honked. Big trucks did the same. A RCMP cop car merely rolled by, flashed its white, blue and red light tree once along with a quick siren blast and slid down the street. A cab stopped and the driver asked if he needed a lift. He said he didn't and took another pull from a crystal liter bottle of Bong Vodka. The stuff was made in Holland. The bottle in Milan Italy. The booze costs about $40 a pop, but Gill's feeling extravagant this night. Good booze and paying for the vodka's boat ride to Canada is worth it right now. The cabbie muttered "Damn Yank drunks" and drove off not all that far behind the squad car.

He looked up and was able to make out the street signs in the ghastly washed-out orange light of the arc streetlights. He discovered that he was lying in the middle of the intersection of 52$^{nd}$ Avenue and 56$^{th}$ Street.

"Not bad," he said to himself. "Not bad at all. I got this far. A little more vodka and a little more rest and I'll head down to the river."

The river was the North Saskatchewan, a river he'd fished many times up near the Rockies casting large streamers for big bull trout and rainbows. The river was still wild. Still full of fight and madness. His kind of country. No rules. Few if any people and lots of grizzlies, moose, eagles, elk, wolverines and ravens. Long-time friends of his. John Wesley had stashed his gear hours ago inside a tent he'd pitched beneath some tall pines at a local park. His truck was parked next to his shelter. Earlier in the day he'd walked up the bluff from the large, aquamarine flow and found his way to Duffer's Pub sitting majestically amidst all the other commercial flotsam that had drifted in on the current high tide of oil-boom Alberta and had washed ashore along the main drag, Highway 11 – Burger King, KFC, Best Western, BP, MacDonald's = in what had once been an out-of-the-way little Canadian Rockies foothills town that was right in the middle of dozens of the finest trout streams anywhere.

"Any fucking where," John Wesley muttered as he took another hit and waved at a group of teenagers that roared by in a battered yellow '69 Super Bee.

"Way to enjoy the night." "Un-fucking-believable." "Yo Dude." "All the way to Calgary, man."

And the car vanished with the roar that only Cherry Bomb mufflers can impart to an internal combustion engine. The smell of exhaust hung on the rainy, still air.

"Haven't seen one of those in a while," he said to the rain.

John Wesley had worked his way down from above the arctic circle in the Yukon at a leisurely pace rolling through, Pelly River, Carmacks, Rancheria, Watson Lake then Fort Nelson and then Dawson Creek in B.C., down through Grand Prairie and Grand Cache where he spent the evening eating and drinking in what used to be a remote mountain outpost but was now a gone-belly-up tourist gig. He slept on the bench seat of the truck. In the morning he bought a large bag of cream-filled glazed donuts and bear claws along with a half-gallon of orange juice. He drank off a pint or so of the juice and replenished the liquid with vodka. He finished off the donuts, half of the now screwdrivers-in-a-carton. He bombed through Hinton along a back dirt road past the Cardinal coalmine that was tearing up the land mountain by mountain on the eastern edge of Jasper National Park. Slogged through muddy, quagmired Forest Trunk 734 all the way to Nordegg. Large oilrigs slid into his path on the Forest Trunk insanity nearly squashing him like an American form of bug. Death was near at hand the entire slip-sliding way. Stacks burning blown off methane from oil drilling glowed filthy orange in the gloom. Clearcuts and open pits left over from strip mining lined the road.

"An abject wilderness hell," John Wesley thought. "Assholes. Alberta's nothing but an extraction industry whorehouse," and he flipped the finger to the entire Canadian Province.

His rig was coated with mud when he hit pavement, but a heavy rain-washed most of the crud away. He did pull over at a campground along the Pembina River and managed to catch a few grayling on elk hairs as he waded the edge of the river casting to seams of current and behind large dark grey rocks. The fish ran and sounded, dorsal fins waving in the current and the air. When he brought the seventeen-inch grayling to him they fluoresced turquoise, deep purple and hardened silver, black spots set the whole display off wonderfully.

He spent a couple of days here fishing and drinking with the campground manager who brought him wood in the back of an old beater Toyota pickup. Canadians took care of their parks, even small, out of the way ones like this little beauty along the tannin stained Pembina whose tea colored waters rushed and swirled over a cobble bottom and whooshed around large midstream boulders. He and the manger would sit around a large fire well into the night trading wilderness experiences.

He recalled a long-ago relationship with a young woman he brought up here once, but was unable to remember her name, how they parted, where she was, if she was even alive. His mind went hazy then blank when he considers these types of moments in his life.

Gill learned a lot about some places to explore up north in the Rockies west of the Smoky River and in the interior chunk of turf between Highway 40 between Grand Cache and Grande Prairie that ran far above this river through grand stands of stately birch and flanked in the east by Highway 43 between Whitecourt and Bezanson. Even with all of the logging, seismic exploration, mining and oil extraction this enormous piece of wild land held countless streams and lakes loaded with grayling, northerns and other fish. Big game was everywhere. And wolves and the biggest ghost all, absolute solitude. Muskeg swamps filled in the low-lying sections. Few people ever ventured into this place according to the manager, and many of those that did often never returned, were never heard from again.

John Wesley liked the sound of this place and made mental plans to go into this pine and birch filled void next summer. Whether he was one of the ones he never returned made no difference to him except to lend some hot spice to the adventure.

The last morning at Pembina he caught some more grayling on long lazy casts and mended drifts. The fish took as the bushy elk hairs swung out and around at the end of the float. Easy and enjoyable fishing.

"Magic Fish, He thought. Then he climbed back in his truck and battled 734 tooth and nail down to Highway 11 and the North Saskatchewan just above Nordegg where the cross-country races were held during the Calgary Olympics long ago.

"Never take that bastard again," he muttered, but

he knew he would. He liked the danger of big trucks plowing their way down the middle of the muddy or blindingly dusty road, their drivers not giving a damn about lesser traffic such as John Wesley. The Forest Trunk road was a free-form test of survival for the unwary or the slightly mad. Take your pick.

Soon he found the park by the North Saskatchewan. He rigged his tent and bed kit before strolling uptown.

He'd spent the afternoon and the early evening working on shots of Whisper Vodka and Shaftebury Four Twenty Brilliant Lager chasers, minding his own business, talking politely when spoken to while watching Australian Rules Football – a crazy game that made no sense, had rules that appeared to change every few minutes and was a swirling mélange of violence, blood, insane fans and even loonier announcers. He watched this loony tunes sport every chance he got.

"I love this game," he always muttered. " Just like life."

He looked out one of the few windows at Duffer's. Noticed the rain and the dark. Hailed the barkeep. Asked for two bottles of Bong. Paid his bill. Then walked out into the surprisingly warm night. This was, after all, Alberta, Canada and, for good measure, three hundred miles up north into the heart of the province.

He strolled along in a fairly drunk good mood taking the back, less-traveled city streets, working on the vodka as he went. Groups of men – two, three, five – were hanging out on various corners smoking cigarettes and passing bottles in brown bags. Gill knew the scene well. He'd been there many times. Lounging around in a standing position shooting the shit about a whole hell of a lot of nothing – baseball, women, politics, money and the lack of it, fishing, whatever – anything to kill off another stultifying, hopeless day. He imagined he'd be with the boys on the corner again in the future. Some patterns never changed and he wasn't a changeable kind of man.

He soon grew weary from the walking and all the booze and the greasy bar food of chicken wings, burgers and onion rings. He belched loudly into the empty drizzling darkness. An old Otis Redding song played a truncated loop in his head. The intersection he now found himself lying in looked as good as any place to take a brief lie down.

John Wesley sat up, rolled over to his hands and knees and stood up, slowly, very slowly. He didn't weave. He never did. He either walked straight as an arrow or fell down flat on his face out for the count. The bottle lay on the street by his Converse All-Star tennis shoes, the jug miles away and only holding a small touch of liquor.

"Fuck it," he said and pulled another from his large coat pocket, wrenched the cap tearing the paper seal and took a deep pull. "That's better."

He found his tent in a few minutes. Unzipped the door and saw that all was well. Gear as he left it. Foam sleeping pad, down sleeping bag and pillow waiting for his touchdown. He lit a Camel straight. Worked on the vodka. Lit another smoke. Worked on the vodka. Lit another. Looked around. Smelled the pine and the wild Rocky Mountains in the rushing, swirling river. He stared at the soft surface glow of the North Saskatchewan and laughed. Something called **night** was working round his head. Scenes from here to Agadir, Morocco to Nanortalik, Greenland to Calgary, Alberta to Casper, Wyoming and finally to spaced-out Livingston, Montana. He'd write this one in the morning over coffee and a little more Bong action.

"Enough of this road shit. Time to head home tomorrow," he thought.

He lit another Camel. Took another hit and laughed again.

Time to head home. Time to head home ...

### night

*neon*

*heart of the night*
*starts beating early*
*like a jazz-crazed demon*
*on the run hard time*
*from previous destinations,*
*where doing the required*
*demanded of all*
*killing brings to life*
*latent anger within*
*a listless flock*
*starts long ago time shuffle*
*when the natural light fades*
*behind the western ridge*
*of busted teeth mountains that shine*
*hot pink, burnt orange*
*buzzed turquoise, crazed chartreuse*
*electric yellow, flame red*
*false gold, bright white*
*Vollmann spectrum*
*all nighttime luminaries*
*showing off their*
*shining reflections*
*bouncing up from the*
*oily puddles*
*left by recent*
*casual thunderstorms*
*casting surreal honest*
*glowing shadings*
*reminiscent of artificial rainbows*

on the boys as they hang lazily out
on the corner by
The Turtle Tap
at Montana and Central
where all the traffic
hooks on by
long legged, tight assed
big breasts, thick makeup
for twenty bucks
in a quarter hour
less if you've got the juice
fired by attractive brilliance
blazing, flashing, winking
above bars, pawns, drug stores, flops
manmade rainbows
artificial radiance
refracting too, too
truthfully abstract failures
committed by those who
tried and failed
arcing and wrapping
around disappointments
enticing and carousing
all night through

landscapes

streets greasy, hot, cracked
skid marked, littered
sidewalks dirty, gumstuck, cigarette butts, spit
fake dollar bill flyers
pimping strip shows swirling in the wind
alleys filthy, dumpsters stinking,
trash bags ripped open
putrid, dead or alive
bodies stinking

*cats, rats, mongrels, humans*
*buildings old, crumbling, soot covered*
*window cracked, decrepit*
*ghost faces behind stained glass*
*sky washed out blue turned*
*smog yellow, brown grey*
*nighttime washed out*
*in atmosphere crud*
*no stars, moon, galaxies, planets*
*flop house old man*
*behind counter*
*in front of keys*
*ratty couches, black-white TV*
*candy machine empty*
*cigarette machine busted*
*ancient People, Time, Sports Illustrated*
*crapped out events*
*from long ago no time*
*JD MacDonald*
*Pale Gray For Guilt*
*on butt burned table*
*thread bare carpet*
*overflowing ashtrays*
*cigar stubs, gum wrappers, toothpicks*
*rooms stink, urine, shit*
*defeat, despair, death*
*wash stand, bed lice, head lice*
*stained sheets, pillowless*
*bare dried out wood floor*
*no curtains, bare lightbulb*
*steam radiator heat*
*yelling, screaming, snoring*
*loud radios, murmurs*
*sleep turned pastime*
*a distant dream*
*hallway closet toilet flushing*

*Plain Crazy in Paradise*

*like bomb going off*
*through rattling pipes*
*shattered mirror*
*stained yellow rust sink*
*shower drips is all*
*tile floor muddied, bloodied*
*walls creaking as bricks*
*cool contract,*
*heat expand*
*payphone in hallway*
*no one to call*

*dreams*

*from that other*
*real world*
*where homes*
*families*
*a twisted sense of security*
*reside beneath*
*manicured lawns*
*some fantasy remains*
*with the bounds*
*of disillusion*
*but being way beyond*
*the ability to dream*
*to even remember*
*what these are*
*while still knowing*
*they exist*
*the awareness*
*causes them pain*
*when they see*
*this hopelessness*
*in the eyes of the*
*innocents*

*cops*

*not many of them mean well*
*thugs, psychotics, sociopaths*
*small minds, envious*
*big mouths masking*
*insecurity building*
*egos run riot*
*riding herd on the streets*
*pigs directing humans*
*like a fascist nightmare*
*in war-torn Watts*
*on the take, running the con*
*unemployable outside the force*
*they thunder along*
*in their squad cars*
*fully loaded, literally*
*high on what they bust*
*looking for trouble that rarely exists*
*except in officious, confused minds*
*that have long gone mad*
*scanning prey that only*
*wants to exist alone*
*without official intervention*
*or societal meddling*
*but cuffs, pepper spray,*
*night sticks, gunfire, tasers*
*perpetual harassment*
*are all part of the drill*
*ask the boys about all this*
*rousted, beaten, shot at*
*busted for vagrancy*
*intoxication, theft, possession*
*big time beef in squint eyes*
*questioned about this*

*threatened about that*
*all of the usual suspects*
*and the cops know*
*that what they're doing*
*improves nothing*
*clogs the system*
*and more to the point*
*fuels a blue boy paycheck*
*that isn't measured in money*
*and does nobody no good*
*fires less than latent urges*
*to put the screws to those*
*who wander slightly lost*
*on all the wrong sides*
*of these exhausted, hell hound*
*streets*

*terror*

*what's a little*
*stark, raving*
*abject fear, horror*
*bugged-eyed madness*
*when the last thirty years*
*have been riddled,*
*shot up the ass*
*into the veins*
*China white style*
*for the foolish*
*sake of running from*
*the clown ghouls*
*that gobble the brain*
*feast on the soul*
*while lunatics in DC*
*bomb the hell out of*
*anyone who disagrees*

*has oil, isn't white*
*drives a camel*
*worships Allah,*
*or the criminally dead*
*tap into what's*
*left of privacy these times,*
*so screaming silently*
*through an internal night*
*that mocks you forever*
*with a sick grin*
*a sardonic laugh*
*that echoes like*
*rabid bats bouncing*
*off skull bones,*
*and is little more*
*than a sadman's*
*dying attempts at*
*trying to remain sane,*
*then even terror*
*has its purpose*

*sensibilities*

*cooling asphalt*
*like kerosene*
*gagging a*
*cool wind*
*auto exhaust*
*chokes, burns*
*grain alcohol*
*slices air*
*stale booze on*
*empty stomachs*
*puke, hunger*
*dissipation*
*roaring buses*

*car horns*
*ripping ears, minds*
*hip-hop-rap-crap*
*feeding hate, frustration*
*transmissions slipping*
*through worn metal*
*like fried joints*
*screeching tires*
*string through a can*
*rough scrape of*
*shoes on concrete*
*rasping like dead grass*
*within drought plains*
*moving within hot, dry wind*
*white port, Tokay*
*sickly sweet on the tongue*
*tasting of saccharine corn candy*
*sweat mixing with dirt*
*on worn out clothes*
*back to stale booze, defeat*
*filth, resignation*
*ambulance, cop sirens*
*all show no hope*
*swirling about with*
*mangled authority*
*whores scream over territory*
*like down-on-their-luck*
*politicians*
*hand on light pole*
*warm metal, rough grime*
*all blending in a vision*
*that spins in washed-out color*
*through drunk eyes*
*external seasons of the*
*lost, sad, judged*

*rats*

*rodents creep out*
*with animal caution*
*like the vermin they are*
*far too close to a subspecies human*
*that brokers lives for wealth*
*at the cost of their souls*
*and the end of others' dreamscape*
*as light dims to stealth*
*hours pass and drunks*
*guzzle, stumble, pass out, are beaten*
*in alleys scarcely lit by*
*dim service entrance bulbs*
*and rats big as terriers*
*move in with yellow*
*razor-sharp fangs*
*gnawing on dissipated flesh*
*clinging to unconscious bones*
*that never feel the creatures*
*ripping and tearing muscle*
*in bloody chunks that*
*drip from ghastly jaws*
*dead is already dead*
*in a lifeless epiphany*
*piercing, glowing eyes*
*scan the scene for*
*predatory intrusion*
*none around so*
*human life is torn from*
*temporal pavement*
*as rat existence flourishes*
*in a black heart landscape*

*violent*

*this one's a jester of sorts*
*not quite what it may seem*
*cause it isn't about rape*
*woman, child nor man*
*in the insane blackness*
*nor screaming crazy in the middle of traffic*
*nor knifings or beatings in dim lounges*
*nor taking out somebody's windshield beneath a streetlight*
*not related to yelling, screaming, swearing in dark rooms*
*mutilating and consuming*
*organs like chamber music*
*trapped within a macabre recital*
*nor flashing the bird*
*nor hate, anger, disgust*
*this one's about the*
*relentless, insidious*
*never forgetting wastings*
*of human dreams*
*women, money, recognition*
*or the real juice —*
*peace, serenity, belief —*
*dreams that lead*
*inside human souls*
*the boys carry the pain of this atrocious*
*long-running humiliation, destruction -*
*all of them smart*
*though not as often as before,*
*consumption takes a toll*
*the booze plays hard here,*
*all of them caring if*
*only a little bit these days -*
*that's where the liquor, drugs*
*chain-smoking comes into play*
*what's a little death trip*

*when you've been*
*killing for years*
*when you've already been*
*beaten senseless for decades*

*loss*

*all of them*
*have experienced*
*the going away*
*that never returns*
*departings of all sorts*
*divorces, fights, emancipations, driftngs*
*one's mother dropped dead*
*while making her*
*nightly old fashioned*
*swizzle stick*
*still in hand*
*smile of shock on her face*
*quick and clean*
*another lost a daughter*
*years back*
*heroin spiked*
*somewhere in Alaska*
*dead end state*
*with bs attitude*
*called tough*
*by weaklings*
*hiding from*
*themselves*
*lost inside*
*ex-wife called*
*let him know*
*he was worthless*
*hung up*
*never saying*

*Plain Crazy in Paradise*

*when the burial*
*would be*
*where it was*
*so he always*
*carries the wonder of it all*
*carved in his scarred heart*
*how cruelty*
*becomes perceived virtue*
*and if perhaps*
*there are flowers on*
*her grave*
*on any grave*

*death*

*the body*
*is lying just*
*up in the alley*
*the body has been*
*lying there for*
*more than a day now*
*splayed form*
*arms legs akimbo*
*holes in soles*
*of shoes*
*cloths filthy, ragged*
*bottle of Muscatel in one*
*grimy hand*
*clutched like*
*a drowning man*
*clinging to a*
*sodden piece of wood*
*trash already piling up*
*like windrows*
*against the corpse*
*flies buzzing*

*John Holt*

*the heat makes*
*things smell like*
*the living dead*
*have come for*
*a visit on the corner*
*one of them*
*decides that he's*
*had enough*
*tells the others so*
*walks into Mickey's liquors*
*calls the cops*
*and comes back out to wait*
*a few hours later*
*a squad shows*
*figuring what's*
*one more dead drunk*
*cloths over noses, mouths*
*they check out the stiff*
*call for an ambulance*
*wait for the arrival*
*oversee the loading of*
*the dead man*
*drive off and*
*everything is back*
*to normal*
*men drinking, smoking*
*hookers hooking*
*pimps hustling*
*junkies nodding*
*death on this street*
*is nothing*
*nothing at all*

*dharma*

*dharma for one*

*Ian Anderson once blew*
*with no awareness*
*no success*
*complete understanding*
*while vainly talking reality*
*grasping at Buddha teachings*
*form, sensation*
*perception, memory*
*consciousness*
*form, no form, form*
*not really close*
*mind empty*
*gone, gone, really gone*
*totally, completely gone*
*perhaps little more than*
*bicameral dreams*
*genetic predispositions*
*pretending dreams*
*skandha aware*
*that is not space*
*emptiness that*
*is not emptiness*
*look for a river*
*find the river*
*again no river*
*in flood stage*
*white jade whipped*
*smashed black dragon pearls*
*avoiding increased flaws*
*then the always outsiders ask*
*without knowing*
*what is*
*what is not*
*receiving answers*
*still uninformed*
*cold moon*

*John Holt*

*high wind*
*no horizon*
*speechless, silent*
*their response*
*forms emptiness*
*lonely is bad*
*being hurt worse*
*giving pain to others hell*
*so the boys dig deep*
*for a change*
*discovering*
*just enough*
*for another bottle*
*that appears full*
*but is not empty*

*blood*

*on the tracks*
*under the bridge*
*spreading, thickening*
*feeding flies, ants*
*as it cooks*
*on the hot*
*pavement where*
*the boys look*
*and see a knife*
*throat stuck*
*in an old drunk*
*with filthy-pants pockets*
*turned out for cash*
*a squad car rolls by*
*two brush-cut pigs*
*look then laugh*
*with hellish obscenity*
*mouths jammed with*

*chewed food*
*they glance again*
*before turning back to*
*crimson-jellied doughnuts*
*black coffee*
*dark like dead blood*
*that smells of*
*counterfeit copper*
*the boys knew the man*
*no one living here*
*is a stranger*
*they watch the squad car*
*fade in morning traffic*
*before placing a bottle*
*half full of bourbon*
*in the dead guy's hand and*
*shove a little money back*
*in his pockets*
*a short funeral of sorts*
*their small caring*
*as they think, know*
*that this is just one*
*gruesome, grisly*
*street that dead ends*
*around the world*

*angels*

*the true beauty*
*is difficult to hide*
*walking on by*
*floating slightly above*
*the hot, cracked sidewalk*
*impossible to describe*
*when a true women*
*the one who sees all of you*

*and with a wise grin*
*flashed your way on waves*
*of pure thought*
*shows you that you're*
*worth getting to know*
*worth helping along the crazy road*
*because she says we,*
*all of crazy us we,*
*truly belong in the*
*white light river paradise*
*that flows way beyond eternity*
*lasting for a forever second*
*and if she really goes on a roll*
*she'll move next to, inside of*
*you, your soul*
*and the boys have been blessed*
*with this rarest of experiences*
*each one of them*
*at least one safe time*
*creating*
*memories that linger*
*long after they*
*have been murdered*
*flourish*
*nourish*
*help*
*keep*
*them*
*alive*

*end game*

*comes on fast*
*the ever-popular*
*brain fade two-step*
*rides in on a very high horse*

nostrils flared, foam-flecked lips, cracked teeth
when the hour shifts to off
dream landscape ghouls dance
pudding thick, drying
blood crazy
on rubber bones
knees turned weak
cadaver ligaments can't hold on
the brain wanders from view
except for skewed vistas
from insane hell
that always lusts unfulfilled
then blacks out
one or two of the boys
a touch less gone
help the others to wherever
safety hides like a stalking cat
in this relentless scene
they've had enough for this day
doing nothing within emptiness
being perceived as even less
requires one hell of a lot
of energy, stamina, guts
when checking out
often makes more sense
so the inevitable shift to
a quiet place of invisibility
those who know don't remember
warehouse, park, alley, abandoned car
ubiquitous dumpster
warmed with paper, food scraps,
cardboard boxes torn up
or maybe if things play well
up on their roof top hideout
if they can crawl that high
fire escape leans out from

*corroded bolts sticking out*
*from rotten brick*
*no Mary Deare wrecks*
*around here in*
*this parched far country*
*naked land*
*soaked in gold*
*foundered*
*run aground again*
*then only then*
*rising on high tide*
*before agonized*
*breaking to pieces*
*to sink among*
*jagged rock islands*
*like mangled bones*
*no, these are definitely*
*the gentlest of touchdowns*
*though still called crash*
*when the dead of night*
*takes over*

# CHAPTER 10
## Searching For Native Color

**SOMETIMES JOHN WESLEY'S** making a failure or success on his own his own terms reshapes his life into a largely disappointing experience. The fact that the Cubs have yet to win a World Series in his lifetime (or his father's or in nearly a century) has become a personal object lesson in perseverance and loyalty. Losing his hair is perceived as a sign of high testosterone levels. And on it goes through convoluted time.

So when Gill set out for the hinterlands of western Wyoming in search of what the Wyoming Game and Fish Department calls the Wyoming-Cutt Slam he had already internally acknowledged that he would probably not catch (and release) the four sub-species of cutthroat trout in question – Yellowstone (*Oncorhynchus clarki bouvieri*), Bonneville (*Oncorhynchus clarki utah*), Colorado (*Oncorhynchus clarki pleuriticus*) and Snake River (proposed classification of *Oncorhynchus clarki behnkei*). If he did succeed he would need to submit a form stating where and when he caught the individual cutthroat along with digital photo documentation of each variety. Then he would receive a color certificate honoring my achievement. There were no expectations on his part concerning fulfilling the Slam, but should this eventuate, he definitely planned on having the full-color certificate framed and hung in a prominent location in his living room or maybe in a bedroom closet.

Gill was never not into competition or quest of any kind. He was initially reluctant to participate in the program, but reading the information on the department's website changed his mind. It stated that the Cutt-Slam is "A program designed to encourage anglers to learn more about Wyoming's cutthroat sub-species and develop more appreciation and support of the Wyoming Game and Fish Department's cutthroat management program." He much prefers native species to introduced gamefish as in casting to the Westslope and Yellowstone cutthroat, mountain whitefish, Montana arctic grayling (*Thymallus arcticus montanus*) and Bull trout as opposed to what most fly fishers prefer chasing – brook, brown and rainbow trout.

So off he went figuring that this elusive cutt-slam novelty item was as good excuse as any to return to the back roads of Wyoming.

Inured to what most psychologically healthy individuals consider abject failure, he figured two, possibly three, species landed would be a rousing success, but had no idea how this peripatetic angling road trip would play out. The slowly realized sinister nature of the adventure may haunt him for the remainder of his life, possibly even threatening the long-term stability of my rock-solid world view.

As he was once again to experience, the angling gods are a capricious and cruel lot.

He headed out for the South Fork of the Shoshone River outside of Cody near the southeastern corner of Yellowstone Park. The road was paved degenerating into gravel winding through development after development then a long-running series of trophy and dude ranches. Once on the Shoshone National Forest every trailhead and turnout was jammed with pickups and SUVs pulling horse trailers. The high country big game season was in full swing. Despite all of this human degradation, the sharp, jagged mountain peaks, escarpments and sawtooth ridges are spectacular especially with a fresh dusting of pure white snow. At the end of the road he stops and works his way up a trail to some passable pocket water. There are excellent pool and riffle stretches all along the way to the parking spot but all of this water is on private land and therefore off limits. This is unlike Montana where an angler can access water from public roads and bridges and wade to his heart's content as long as he stays within the high water marks. In Wyoming water that flows through private holdings is **PRIVATE!** No exceptions. Montanans tend to take this freedom for granted, but it is truly a gift not to be squandered or given up to out-of-state wealthy who have accumulated a massive war chest in an attempt to overturn the state's stream access law. Not on Gill's watch. Not while he's still kicking. Signs, padlocks, link chains, and metal gates have all experienced Gill's brand of justice - .357 magnum rounds, locks flash-frozen by spraying them with up-side-down cans of photographer's air and then shattered with a ball peen hammer, gates run through and run over and so forth.

He's packed a number of specialty rods that he doesn't use all that much but treasures all the same. For the South Fork he rigged up an Orvis 6-0', one-ounce, two-weight - a deceptively strong and accurate rod. Lightweight rods are a delight on small streams such as this one as long as the fish are played quickly so that they are not exhausted to the point of dying. Attached to the end of a 4x tippet is a Royal Wulff. The first four casts to likely looking holes produce small Yellowstone cutts that run in splashing circles briefly then came splashing to his wet hands. Then he photographs the little guys with a compact digital camera before turning them free.

The South Fork is far too residential and locked up

for Gill's wild tastes so he decides to cut the fishing short and move on down the road. Since he has a long distance to cover for the next chapter of this cutthroat adventure somewhere in the southwestern part of the state he plans on chewing up some highway miles after a snack of sharp white cheddar, sausage, sour dough bread and orange juice.

Despite the beauty of the day and the landscape, subdivided as it is, shadowy, chill intimations disturbing in nature dance among the steep, bouldered and timbered valleys to the east. Gill feels uneasy. Danger on the rocks is surely here, somewhere. This quest that seems to be morphing into a seriously perverse Bass Masters meat hunt (possibly a slight example here of verbal overkill - on second thought, not really) in his 'capricious little mind,' he says out loud as he finishes this latest thought riff. 'What the hell. I'm easily lead astray and often proud of it, so play on.'

After marveling at the rock walls and cliffs studded with myriad rock formations that towered over the emerald Wind River below Thermopolis, he spends a full-moon night along the sandstone-crested shore of a west-central Wyoming reservoir. At sunrise he hits the road early then manages to kill a week or two waiting for coffee at a kiosk staffed by individuals more interested in making their own specialty concoctions than waiting on paying customers. Then the road climbs up over the southern end of the Wind Rivers glowing in autumn aspen saffron, before drifting lazily past the tourista mining and Oregon Trail townsites of Atlantic City and South Pass City. The day is high altitude, clear blue, late September. Antelope by the hundreds graze, laze and stand casually in the sage flats. He roams the high desert making his way to the town of Kemmerer, home of the original J.C. Penney's store. Gas is cheap here and the residents are friendly – a delightful combination. He loads up on food and fuel and heads out west northwest towards a river drainage of isolated and obscure dimensions. Turning up a narrow paved road that turns quickly to gravel and dirt he sees the tributary we are looking for – a perfectly clear sapphire stream twisting like a sensual snake through golden yellow and orange stands of aspen, willow and alder. Angus and Hereford stand dumbly beneath the still warm sun. Eagles glide. Hawks circle above soon-to-be-dead rabbits. Mule deer hold on steep sage-pocked slopes. Rounded mountains topped with new snow bend off into the distance. This is paradise in Gill's often-jaded eyes.

He drops down a steep rocky two-track to the stream, sets up camp and heads to the water. Beautiful water it is – riffles, runs, pools, undercut banks but after hours of casting all there is to show are a missed one-foot Bonneville and the vanishing sight of three tiny trout fleeing for their lives at his approach. He walks back to camp somewhat perplexed but not discouraged. Tomorrow will see him through. A grilled ribeye and baked potato dinner eaten as the full-moon rises over a steep ridge reinforces this optimism and resolve. Strong black coffee laced with sugar and thick cream drunk within a sparkling sunrise frosty morning furthers his determination.

Moving along the road a piece, sliding through a steep cutbank of rock, sage and small cactus Gill works his way upstream for perhaps a half-mile with no luck. Hare's ear nymphs, Elk hair caddis, Royal Wulffs, BWOs – all to no avail. He's noticed grasshoppers clacking and crash landing in the roadside grasses yesterday and begin to hear them as the day grows warmer. Tying on the rattiest one he has, then greasing the sucker down to make sure it rides high and dry, he launches it to the head of a long, wide, deep aquamarine pool. The bug lands with a "plop." I can smell the slightly creosote scent of the sage as it heats up. A warm breeze slides downstream. A few clouds ride the wind. Magpies and crows argue over something rotten on a nearby rise. The water burbles over and around the cobbled streambed that flashes bright earthy shades of red, tan, ochre, grey and green. The fly drifts slowly to me when I spot an open mouth, white inside of jaws clearly visible as a Booneville rises slowly from the river's bottom following the hopper in near-vertical position for five, six feet before taking the bait.

At the set of the hook, the trout runs and leaps for twenty feet, then sounds and runs some more before breaking the surface in a spray of crystal to jump for the light several more times. The fish comes to him struggling at this indignity and assault on its natural freedom. He holds the trout and wonders at its design, its colors and its similarity to Yellowstone cutts, then takes a bunch of photos before the fish is turned loose, disappearing in the green-blue depths. Two more casts produce two more cutthroat like the first one and the day is made and he's happy. Back at the Suburban he drinks a couple of cans of crème soda, eats sausage and cheese and rides a fine day for all it's worth, one of the finest, growing better by the moment.

As with all road trips, out of the ordinary is par for the course. On the walk back to the rig three stoned, blasted Bozos stop and ask him where to gain access to the water. They're in a painting company truck from Jackson if the logos stuck to the side of the rig mean anything. The guy in the back obviously lost track of his name weeks ago and has contented himself with working on a can of Schlitz beer. They tell Gill they've caught a hundred Bonnevilles and plenty of

Czechoslovakian browns with blue stripes above their eyes. The driver tells him they were planted over two hundred years ago. John Wesley looks this crew over, chats a bit and then they vanish in a cloud of dust. He doesn't see any fishing gear in the cab or the truck's bed. Never heard of blue-streaked eastern European browns and if their planting data is correct the *salmo trutta* described here were dropped in this little stream before Lewis and Clark wandered westward.

Ah, yes. The joys of conversing with the terminally wasted. He fully understands the concept. Gill laughs while a turkey vulture offers a widespread wing display on a weathered fence post. The behavior is known as a horaltic pose whose purpose is to bake off parasites, dry feathers and warm the body. A companion looks on with obvious boredom. These creatures defecate on their own legs, using the evaporation of the water in the feces and/or urine to cool themselves down. There's a fancy scientific name for this, but considering the ostentatious nature of the behavior using the word might be overkill. The vultures also projectile vomit on perceived enemies. Wonderful creatures, every one of them.

Last night he met a woman in a Kemmerer bar and took her back to camp – drinking, talking and finally the heart of the matter, screwing. When he woke at sunrise she was gone. No sign of her remained at his camp along the small river.

"Where'd she run off to?" he asks himself. The land has no reply. It's gone silent. "Maybe she was never here. The booze most likely," and he shakes his head, smiles and says out loud, "Fat chance. She was here."

While finishing his snack, Gill makes plans to head for the upper Green River to seek Colorado cutthroat tomorrow morning.

The drive up to an open, grassy flat on the Green

River a few miles below Green River Lakes in the Bridger Wilderness is pleasant, scenic and uneventful. He sets up camp and decides to enjoy the snow-crested peaks of the Wind River range while cooking dinner. There'd be plenty of time to catch Colorado cutts tomorrow and the next day or so he thought. Flat Top Mountain dominated the skyline as it passed through grey-indigo, lemon, orange and then darkening lavender color phases as the sun dropped from the sky.

The next day he fishes the river for a couple of miles catching plenty of 8-12 inch wild rainbows. Beautiful fish but not the cutts we are after. For some reason Gill's growing anxious about this and not really enjoying himself like he normally does when fishing. Most curious. He decides to hike into the wilderness along the eastern shore of the lower of the lakes. The wind is severe from the south whipping whitecaps and blowing leaves from the aspens in a steady stream as he works his way several miles to Clear Creek. The stream pours over a natural barricade of granite, plummeting 89 feet to form a shallow pool and then races down hill through a rocky streambed to join the Green. Flakes of iron pyrite (fool's gold) sparkles among the dark shoreline sands.

Royal and Green Humpies turned numerous small rainbows colored intensely in purple, crimson, dark green and silver with black spotting and bluish parr marks along the flanks, but again no Colorados.

"I thought for sure they'd be in this stream if anywhere," he says to himself. "I don't get it. This is crazy."

Look at the light playing off the waterfall," another part of his mind says. "Isn't it beautiful? What a great day."

"Yeah. Right," he continues all the while wondering where he'll find a Colorado cutt so he can complete this portion of the Slam. He realizes that this pursuit is taking over his outlook on things and spoiling the joy of fishing, but those are minor considerations at this point. There is a goal here that needs to be met. Gill's obsessed. Driven. Fame and silliness are riding on each cast. The tension is growing, becoming thick, palpable. Can he do this? The imagined crowd looks on in studied silence.

He fishes for a couple of hours taking lots of colorful rainbows but no Colorados cutthroats, then heads back to camp, an enjoyable exercise in the late afternoon sun that warms him, illuminates the dense pine forest across the lake and highlights mountains that rip skyward all over the place.

He decides to drive back down south to Big Piney and work the South Piney Creek and its tributary, the Landers Fork. Sage flats and bluffs dotted with oilrigs and storage facilities dominated the landscape as we head into the Wyoming Range. John Wesley's growing restless not catching the Colorado cutts and even a bit grumpy. He understands that he's succumbed to a variation of competition fishing and doesn't like the sensation. Competitive fly fishing and one-fly contest lunacy rising in his head like mountain whitefish in the middle of large feeding browns.

'Enough. Enjoy the rainbows from yesterday, the country I'm passing through and the fishing that awaits me.'

At the Landers Fork he rigs up a unique five-foot, two-weight rod made by Damon Fly Rods – ideal for small, brushy streams like this one. Lots of decent casts to pools and pockets. No fish of any stripe. The same holds true lower down on the South Piney in larger water that is as pretty as any he's seen. Fishless all the same.

One last shot will be along Highway 189 as he aims

north towards Jackson. At the bridge that spans Cottonwood Creek he gets out of the Suburban and peers into the weedy creek. There are a dozen or more Colorado cutthroat. He only wants one so he rushes back to grab his rod when he notices a large silver Dodge Ram Parked on a ridge above us. Driver's-side window rolled down. Gill can clearly see a henchmen – no doubt a common laborer for the nearby (and as he now notices posted) trophy ranch – monitoring him with a pair of large binoculars. Confrontation, harsh words, fisticuffs, gunfire loom on the ugly horizon. Gill is up to all of this, but decides to pass and move on. Lucky for the ranchhand flunky.

'The hell with it.'

And for some reason the mad compulsion to accomplish the Cutt-Slam goes away. Just like that. Gone. He feels a putrid load of tension rise from my shoulders and blow away on a western wind. Gill grins at the world. Life is better now.

He pulls back onto 189 and heads north and politely waves at the gentle soul in the Dodge as he passes. No Colorado cutthroat trout. No Cutt-Slam certificate this year, but there's still the legendary fine-spotted Snake River subspecies to chase. Soon he's in the headwaters of the Hoback River and not long after he's well up a gravel road and camped alongside a fair-sized tributary. Night is setting in so he makes dinner, enjoys a fire and hot tea before turning in.

The morning breaks sunny and clear. The stream rushes and burbles past the campsite. Steam rises from the water seeming to fluoresce in the light. After coffee he rigs up and begins casting a Royal Wulff to all likely holding locations. At a large pool that holds tight to a house-sized boulder a fish rises swiftly to the fly, sets itself, leaps and thrashes before coming to shore. A small Snake River cutthroat covered in hundreds of tiny jet black spots. He plays the fish briefly before it.

A fine morning, a great trip that was nearly ruined by his juvenile need to complete the Slam of slams. As he motors through eastern Idaho on the way home to Livingston running just west of the backside of the Tetons through aspen groves and pine forest he looks back on all of the fish he's caught on the trip – Yellowstone, Bonneville and Snake River cutthroat and those beautiful rainbows. And stores away the object lesson dealing with the idiocy of competitive fly fishing.

The miles roll by as we wind down the Gallatin Valley. The day is gorgeous, light, color and landscape dancing together in perfect harmony. Gill's thoughts run from how the Cubs are doing and how his home is … Oh Boy! … how 'I'm going to call a Wyoming fisheries biologist next year about where would be prime Colorado cutthroat water. Where may I expect to take this elusive sub-species? I need that full-color certificate hanging on my living room wall.'

Gill pulls over alongside the upper Gallatin to fish some and spend the night by the river. After catching rainbows and brookies – unlike the cutthroat of his quest, these two are non-natives, foreign species to this country – he sits down by a small fire and watches evening come with its deepening purples.

What can be said other than a fool and his desires are a tragic combination as the following riff Gill wrote after wolfing down scrambled eggs and fried calf brains mildly explains.

### casting about

*convincing the big boys to take*
*is even harder than they tell you*
*matching the hatch jive doesn't get it*
*nor does artful casting over classic water*
*with a dainty piece of pretentious fluff*

*the ones that matter, those worth the effort*
*will never buy the obvious con of this artifice*

*learning to see without looking*
*understanding how to chase without wanting*
*makes hammering an offering of substance*
*tight to a sweet lie just barely possible*
*with laughable stealth and silent humor*

*now damn it, why would anyone*
*want to do any of this to begin with*

# CHAPTER 11

## Prairie Fire, Northerns and Denny Rehberg

And it's small town talk, it's a well-known fact
You don't ever know how one might react
To what you're thinkin' ...
> *- Small Town Talk* by Bobby Charles

**BERNARD HILL 8'6" BAMBOO ROD**, seven-weight line, short leader, heavy streamer blown all to hell and sometimes back, hard back into my head. Wind blasting and gusting across high plains openness and cold. Classic empty-land northern pike turf - small, little-known, little-fished water sometimes full of fierce predators that gorge on forage fish, a few wayward rainbows, birds that fly too low to the ground, small mammals. Stream surface ragged frothing with beaten-down whitecaps from the storm. The pike are holding in holes only they know. Not much luck, one three-pound pike, but a wild ride none-the-less when the line looped over a wild rose bush and the wind tugged the line and the northern began levitating head first into the sky before the tippet snapped on a thorn. Still he keeps casting while being slammed around by the weather and the streamer.

Earlier a hundred yards from this small stream with the word river in its name while he sat warming up in the Suburban on the side of a chewed up remnant of a narrow paved road, a frigid rancher pulled up on his ATV heading to home warmth after dealing with his cattle. Hoody and Carhartts.

"What're you doin' out here," he asked with a grin. "You must be crazier than I am to be out here. Hell, you'd think it was late November." It was late

September

Gill looked at two columns of smoke that resembled twin bomb blasts that were billowing high to the east, northeast. After a few thousand feet of altitude the gale sheared the tops off the plumes and sent the smoke on its way to the Dakotas.

"Some dumb ass was burning something across the border. Now his property is toast. They're evacuating the town."

He'd had wondered at all of the emergency rigs roaring past us as he neared the Alberta border as we watched the smoke explode sky high. Flashing lights. Siren screams. Emergency crews in full regalia. Nervous, determined expressions on the faces of the firefighters.

"Glad the wind's going away from here." The rancher turned to spit with the wind, tobacco juice sailing away in a long brown string.

John Wesley agreed with him. Wildfire out here is a death trip in a hurry when prairie fire races over the dry land at sixty mph like an enormous, flaming clipper ship gone berserk. Incinerated sage grouse, torched mule deer, charred humans left in its still-life wake. Perhaps a metaphor of sorts for John Wesley's life.

"Northerns still in there?" John Wesley asked while looking at the water than snaked deep blue back and forth through small cut banks covered in rust colored grasses that rippled like frantic waves in the blow.

"Oh yeah. Lots of 'em." He spread his gloved hands about three feet apart. "Thick as logs. Eat damn near anything including the ducks. Don't expect much in all this," and he waved a hand at the wind as clumps of tumble weed bounded past our rigs. "Fish will be holding under the banks where they can."

"Mind if I fish here?"

"Have at it. I'm going home for a drink in front of the wood stove."

He smiled, waved and roared off, soon lost behind a rise the crumbling pavement climbed over.

Maybe the northerns are still here, but would not respond to the streamer the few times it found the water and not my back or thick tangles of wild rose. He'd caught them years ago up to a dozen pounds. Voracious fish that slashed through the shallows or appeared like submerged rockets from dark nowhere. He'd come all the way up here from Yellowstone country to try again despite knowing that autumn winds would make this difficult. Make that impossible.

Gill finished up taking photographs with a pocket Pentax camera he always carried on trips like this one, snapshots of the stream, the severe landscape and the fire blasting away in the distance - a documentation of sorts of where he's been, where's going, what he plans on doing. He forced the door open and piled in, his face red from the cold and wind. He decided to head back to Cutbank and find a motel room.

This quickly degenerated from a simple task turned difficult with the arrival of Republican Senate candidate and Montana's lone member of the House of Representatives. Denny Rehberg who was in a fight as fierce as this weather with Democratic incumbent John Tester. Both men were stereotypical bought-and-paid for political hacks, but Tester, riding the crest of his just-plain-folks crew-cut, was the marginally lesser of the two evils; though I admired Rehberg's forthright candor concerning his self-absorption and venality. As an example, there's the pepper-haired and mustachioed Rehberg suing Billings firefighters not so long ago for opting to save homes from a fire in 2008, including his, while neglecting to save his shrubs on land he planned to develop. The harried responders raced frantically about saving homes at the expense of Rehbergs shrubbery. Denny was not amused. He filed a lawsuit. The taxpayers of Billings were forced to spend $20,761 defending the men from the candidate's legal shenanigans. But with Denny it's me first all the time and that's what really counts here. He makes no bones about this and in this way he's at least being honest while Tester mouths "Power to the common man," jive only the foolish buy into. But then, that's politics. Six weeks later he was despondent when Tester narrowly retained his seat in Washington. Rehberg is back tending to his new shrubbery. Life is unfair sometimes as we learned when trying to find a room to spend the night.

His favorite motel, right out of the late fifties and located near a 25-foot talking Penguin statue, try starting the day hung over and half blitzed dealing with this, was full as were two others. He'd seen Rehberg dressed in Wal-Mart off-the-rack jeans, shirt, bolo tie, Navy-blue sport coat only one size too small and a knock-off Stetson standing alongside his large bus greeting and glad handing the faithful and terminally subnormal in a park nearby. The new or late-model bus glistened with a recent wax job reminiscent of Rehberg's action in Congress last year. And the machine was festooned with jingoistic platitudes, the candidate's name and other important stuff. This slick election device only costs between $2,000 and $3,400, so his contributors are getting a true Montana bargain for their money. Apparently his fan base follows him from town to town along the highline that is the U.S. 2 corridor booking blocks of rooms well in advance.

As a last resort Gill went in to a Super 8 on the western edge of town. Before registering, he rummaged around for a Trinidad Reyes cigar, a pint of whiskey and watched oilfield rough necks pull in from the fields and congregate in small groups while drinking from cans of Ranier and puffing cigarettes, all except a lone black men who climbed out of a Dodge Crew Cab, walked away from the other men and worked on a pint of brown liquor while smoking a cigar and staring off into the distance of where he'd just been. Life in Montana, real Montana, hasn't changed all that much in the last century. The tableau playing out in front of him said it all.

The rooms, decorated in early-American bomb-shelter, were $92 each. John Wesley I said "The hell with that." I mean a Super 8 at close to a hundred bucks. Maybe 40 or even 50 but not 100. Gotta love the political arena and the oil business. The economy up here hums on the madness. At least he told the man at the desk, he said, "Take it or leave it" with a I don't give a damn one way or the other expression. John Wesley left it and pushed through the glass doors at the entrance out into the wind.

He decided to run down along the Front hoping to score a place for the night in someplace like Bynum, Dupuyer or even Choteau.

The wind kicked up a notch and the roughnecks went inside except for the lone figure rocking back and forth as he worked over his liquor.

Leaving Cutbank was a relief. He rolled along the mountainous Front, the wind uncommonly absent. Deer, antelope, cattle and fence-sitting raptors monitored our passing. Ranch lights winked on here and there. The sun was wiped out by a dark bank of storm clouds holding above the mountains as it was hopefully setting behind the Rockies of the Bob Marshal Wilderness. The sky was filling with stars that glowed like miniature headlights, or maybe even like alien spacecraft. Gill worked on a Styrofoam cup of coffee, lost in his own thoughts. Gradually the slightly unnerving, though familiar sensation of what most people refer to as déjà vu overwhelmed him. He considered the experiences to be more along the lines of connecting with parallel trips or riffs through non-linear time. Not memories of past lives despite being convinced that I was former PGA tour veteran Charlie Sifford somewhere in the past. He liked his cigars, was a loner and could putt like a demon in John Wesley's youth so maybe he was the gruff man. Soon one part of his mind was keeping the Suburban between the lines cruising at a stately 65 mph while another facet roamed the airwaves ...

### Long time running

*God the wonders keep coming*
*Living in some of the best of it all*
*Fools obsess with playground insecurity*
*Nothing of importance*
*Like shutting down a chainsaw*
*Or sending Conrad home*
*Maybe blowing apart a pump jack*

*Oh no, none of that silliness*

*We got us here a bunch of clowns*
*Who think they're big-time artistes*
*And they want all of us to know*
*How long they've been around*
*Pretending they're all real Montana cool*
*Upwards of twenty-five years one of them*
*Smirks with hooked beak upturned*
*While he dashes off pricey*
*Faded color assembly line scenery*
*That the way-too-rich snap up*
*like hungry browns during hopper time*

*Yeah and I got drunk with Brautigan says one*
*And I passed out in a gutter in '87 brags another*

*This is big-time stuff*
*Ranking right up there*
*With grade school turf wars*
*Playing Cowboys and Indians*
*Or Captain Kangaroo and Tom Swift*
*Which loosely translates into*
*Raging insecurities manifesting*
*Themselves as little kids*

*Yeah and I lived in Missoula more than thirty years ago*
*Back when that town was a town*
*And not an overrun madhouse*
*That has nothing to do with Montana*
*Back when the spring kegger laced with Oly and acid*
*And no one knew Rock Creek, Bitterroot, Clark Fork tunes*
*Lost Highway, Mission Mountain Wood, The Top Hat*
*Midnight runs on the Circus pinball machine at Eddie's*
*Mescaline and champagne trips to Squaw Tit Peak*

*And I hung out in Whitefish when it was still a mountain town*
*Norton Buffalo, Swift Creek, The Palace, The Viking*
*One golf course, no gated communities, no Hummers*
*Instead of a yupster-second-home-ski-crazed-golf-course-raped*

*Plain Crazy in Paradise*

    *Hell hole that I no longer remember*

    *So the fuck what?*
    *We all are to blame for the goodbye to the best of*
*it*
    *Me as much or more than most*
    *Whether we've hung around for thirty-five years,*
*a hundred or a summer*
    *Nowhere time scales vindicating insecurity*
    *No value, nowhere, at no time*

    *But really, none of this silliness*

    *Necessary costumes required*
    *Black bandanas, Bowie knives, full camo*
    *Riding a psycho violence threat*
    *To buy a little deserved space*
    *From a long-dead now cold war*
    *That can't be dropped*
    *While terrorizing effete and fragile*
    *Wandering sidewalk fare*
    *Which can use the scaring*
    *But all the same;*
    *Or silly hats and other affectations*
    *Because man I been on the scene*
    *Yeah all those artistes*
    *Figured this one out early on*
    *Fake the talent and run the con*
    *Mooches buy damn near anything*

    *Mountain, river, prairie*
    *Ponderosa, sage, prickly pear*
    *Wind, sun, rain*
    *Seasons, years, eons*
    *Grayling, cutthroats, bull trout*
    *Grizzly, coyote, elk*

*Meadowlark, Red tail, magpie*
*Space, freedom, sanity*

*We're all way too hip for all this silliness*

... John Wesley came back to his current earthly domain as he pulled into Choteau after dark. He was beat from 700 miles of driving and needed to hit the recline button. The lights of the town seemed welcoming but there were no rooms to be had. Oil exploration along the Front and work at existing oil fields has led to an influx of roughnecks like in Cutbank. The few motels were full up. he was wondering where to go next – Augusta? or perhaps pulling over at the city park and sleeping in the back of the Suburban. Plenty of room. He'd done this many times, but visions of a local cop rousting him at 3 a.m. danced in his head. He noticed a sign for camping and cabins so he turned left at a stop sign near the Roxy Theater and drove to the place on the east edge of town, went in the office and then came out a few minutes later talking and laughing with a woman who was the owner. He'd secured a small cabin with a double and bunk beds for less than thirty bucks. Rustic in a good way with no bedding so he used his down bags and slept the sleep of eternal daydreamers waking to a frosty morning. He used the empty communal showers, had breakfast downtown and decided to retrace his steps to some degree. The plan was to slip through Great Falls and over the Belt Mountains fishing to a small stream on the far side. The wind kicked up midmorning and was soon howling as he approached Fairfield.

A large column of smoke was angling to the east towards Great falls being pushed by the icy wind roaring down from the mountains 50 miles away. Gill was worried about being caught in a wildfire and sped up, exceeding the speed limit by 20 mph. John Wesley wanted out of here. Just ahead he spotted a large, bus gleaming in the ephemeral sunlight.

"Oh God!" he thought. "Not Denny again."

He flashed on yesterday and felt that odd sense of disorientation seeping into my head.

"Not this time," he said determined to focus on his escape.

"What are you talking about," a voice in his head asked, the one that was always lurking on the fringes of his thoughts when he did things that he sometimes wished he could take back.

"Just babbling to myself, buddy," he thought.

"Okay," the voice said.

As he drove past the bus he noticed that the machine was painted blue and white with something like "Go Eagles" plastered on its sides. Similar to Rehberg's rig but different enough to ease my anxiety. The fire turned out to be an old shed flaming away under the watchful eyes of the local fire department. Thick hoses were dousing the perimeter of the flames with sprays of silvery-white water. Even in this wind the situation appeared under control. I felt much better.

He motored on, caught lots of small Yellowstone cutthroat on soft hackles in a forested creek sheltered from the weather by large pines and reached home at sunset. He unpacked food, clothes and rods leaving the rest for a future excursion. He remembered that there was an all-day marathon of *Destination Truth* on the SyFy channel today. A solid dose of reality TV style sounded good. Josh Gates would bring him home.

"Déjà vu my ass," John Wesley said.

"Now what?" the voice asked.

"Nothing, buddy. Nothing at all."

# CHAPTER 12

## Familiar Country

**A BASIC BENCH** of elongate, north-south dimensions offers vistas of unimagined elegance. Aging, rounded mountains marked by spare copses and wavering bands of weathered Ponderosa hold the northern sky. Native grasslands, dry alkali lake beds, deep green ponds filled with spring-fed, sweet water and ringed with dying cattails, desiccate coulees choked with Russian thistle, and eroding bluffs that look like paws of immense panthers drift away in the other three compass directions. Farther off, east, the Little Rockies shine golden orange in the softening light of late afternoon. Several antelope work easily along the side of a brown swale a mile down from this place, black-masked faces working alertly up and down as their white rumps tag along. Fifty yards away mule deer noisily paw at the ground searching for moist Blue grama roots through a mat of dead grass, wind-blown pine needles, cones and white-grey dust. A soft breeze rises up the far side of this rise in a forgotten moan, wanders across the flat carrying the remains of summer's heat, then blows up above me in a quick push that dies out below small tufts of cloud that thin perceptibly from the event. This hemisphere is gradually turning its back on the sun for now. The star appears to have shifted down south - merely a case of human arrogance waging its futile battle with the constancy of its life source. A subconscious attempt to control what is little understood, feared. This light's angle of incidence is flatter, now slanting through the air as a mixture of amber, gold, yellow and crimson. Looking at the landscape is like seeing the world through a crystal tumbler of the finest bourbon gentled slightly with spring water, perhaps from nearby ponds. None of the other days in the year compare to these finely-tuned wonders of late September and early October, not the bright green explosions of spring or the hot gems of summer or the soft white mysteries of deep winter. There is a perfection here, an essence distilled to intense yet subtle radiance that always makes me wonder if I'm still traveling across the same planet I now barely recall from just a couple of months past - late July and its parched heat mixed with wildfire smoke. Was that part of this world? Was it real?

Next-day-waking on this bench, tarp-pad-sleeping bag for a bed, as the sun rises above the distance of the Little Rockies, the eastern horizon goes from black to silver to variations of reds and orange before the skyline blazes in light too intense to quantify with colorful names. The brilliance temporarily silences mourning doves calling to each other from nearby trees. Even a raucous trio of ravens cuts its jive. The intense display causes an opposite effect among the cattails down below as dozens of red-winged blackbirds fire salvos of their wildly electric calls back and forth. Crimson wing bands that are this species' hallmark glow in the new day's radiance. Indigo shadows cast by mountains and bluffs that at first stretched, undulated for hundreds of yards across the rough prairie, visibly withdraw looking like phantasmic arms during the sun's ascension, as though they are being drawn back into that distant nuclear source that now dominates everything out here. Frost that cast prismatic reflections during first light turns to clear droplets hanging from the seed tops of the sere grass, crystalline rainbow colors flash miniature magic in the air. This moisture soon becomes faint steam. Then it's gone, the land dry once again.

The day warms, moves along. Coffee, orange juice, a couple of dry bagels before packing water, sourdough, cheese, summer sausage, apples, shotgun shells – 20-gauge, larger fly patterns like buggers, Sheep Creeks, miniscule dries of no name and personal design, extra tippet, grabbing the Berretta over-under in oiled sheepskin and canvas case slung over shoulder, a one-ounce-two-weight in black tube doubling as walking stick, then side hilling and sliding down the grassy slope to the ponds scattered like favored emeralds across the pink, ochre, slate, purple of the exposed flats and eroding faces of the hills. Several miles away a wall of buff-colored sandstone winds around the top of a rocky dome looking like the ramparts of a castle long abandoned by those who once valued isolation and remote purity. Hundreds of feet below this are many acres of green watered by a buckled-pipe sprinkling system that shoots spray and sporadic gouts of water across domesticated grass. Timothy? Alfalfa? Whoever is doing this is out of sight, vanished. The only signs of habitation are a crumbling assemblage of homestead buildings – brown-to-grey wood frame home, log out buildings - and a few pieces of rusting machinery that was new in the twenties. Scanning through binoculars, gnarled crabapple trees show their beaten trunks rising above cracked soil, the small fruit deep orange marked with charcoal imperfections.

Passing along the first pond, electric blue damselflies zip through the cattails or hover inches above the glassy surface of dark water. The brief morning breeze, cool but holding seams of the mid-day warmth to come, is gone. The air is still. Small mayflies rise crazily into the air along the edges of a spring that bubbles a few feet from shore. Small fish splash after them. The dark shapes of smallmouth bass, large fish, no doubt planted by the invisible rancher, cruise the edges of the cattails feeding on the damsel and mayfly nymphs/larvae and the smaller fish, the white of their open mouths visible as they slash at angles when feeding. There will be time to take a couple of these on the return back up the rise to the bench. That's later. In another time.

Several hundred yards beyond all of this the ground appears parched, crusted with off-white salts. Stepping onto this, my boots sink into clinging jet-black mud turning a twenty-foot crossing into an effort. On the far side is a trail of prints, four-toed, wide pad, the track of a large cat, pressed inches into the moist earth. They lead to the mountains, eventually disappearing amid the clumps of bunch grass that grow, barely, in the baked, rocky dirt. A discarded skin from a milk snake is impaled on prickly pear spines, the membrane shriveled from exposure, the formerly vibrant bands of red, black and white now lifeless, opaque parodies of the real thing. The animal must have used this open place to shed its scaly covering before sliding off to hide beneath a rotting log nearby while its new skin hardened. Glassing the hills shows a band of elk working up towards a pocket of trees in a small crease that probably holds some water.

Looking to the northwest the sky holds so blue it approaches black. An hour of this walking, often punctuated with the strong aroma of crushed juniper branches that block the way, creates a rhythm that is natural, appropriate to this day and this landscape. With temperatures climbing to seventy, soon higher, the last of this season's grasshoppers spring into action, making lengthy, clacking leaps from grass stem to bare rock to sage brush. A pair of Western meadowlarks dives bush-top level snaring some of the slower, smaller insects. The black-and-white of a skunk is visible as the animal abandons its normal nighttime routine this time of year to root among stones and moss surrounding the moistness of an ephemeral spring. I angle away from the busy thing aiming for a cut in the cliffs that leads to a creek holding tiny brook trout. Sharp-tailed grouse always hold beneath the flattened stands of juniper that grow on either slope. The trout are too small to eat, but the brookies' colors glow at this spawning time in their lives. A grouse or two, a couple of the bass, a little bourbon around a reasonable fire, a cigar. A casual touch down to end the day. Sitting on a slab of sandstone that broke away from the cliff above centuries ago, I eat some sausage, cheese, fruit, drink a little water. A mile or two to go. The grouse kick up at my approach and I mark where they land for the return in a few hours. (The word "I" is used in this, but there is no longer any pretense regarding identity or the self-important "I." When far out this way coasting solitaire, nothing matters any more. A bothersome, self-absorbed ego is shed like the snake did with its skin. "I" is merely narrative artifice here.)

*An artifice of little value beneath this sun with no one to see me.*

Perhaps and anon, I chatter to the voice as I often do these days, talking out loud becoming a high art as my time passes. Then play on, I mutter, on to the tiny fish and later some dead birds for dinner, I say to the shadowed soarings of several dozen gregarious Swainson's Hawks winging their way to winter in South America. A rare sight, indeed. Quite strange, but then as they say ... when you're a stranger ... and while we're at it, who the hell needs whiskey these days and a chorus of plaintive *krees* issue from the soaring *Buteo* migration.

*Kree it is then. Continue on Gill. You're mad as a hatter and growing much better at this latest illusion. No death in this one just yet.*

As it should be and thoughts of not-needed whiskey consumed around tonight's essential fire run circle round my head. We, my voices and I, continue on through the gap leading to the brook trout while groups of sharptails break from dense cover at our approach in a lunatic cacophony of guttural clucks, cackles and frantically beating wings. Mad as I can be and happily drifting through this intense fall paradise that I've yet to fall from, graceful or otherwise.

Hours later and the day's gone dark, but the sky is riddled with stars that have dropped down to ground level, surrounding me in a special silver glow that is further heightened by the ghosting green of the northern lights. The tiny brook trout that I caught on #24 dries, fish the size of my index finger, linger in my vision like brightly-colored, high-caliber bullets of blood red, cerulean, white, black, orange and on and on. These hues matching the explosion of colorings that ripped from the ground, the sage, the bluffs, the coulees, the sky when the sun touched the western horizon not all that long ago. That's when coyotes all around me launched insanely happy choruses of barking, howling and syncopated sounds I'd never heard before, continuing on with the jazz-like madness until a crescent moon made an appearance. The animals stilled, their talk replaced with the boomings of night owls working the air for bugs. I climbed the rise to camp tired and truly at peace, an uncommon deal when back in town.

The grouse are split in half, lightly seasoned and roasting on a grill over a modest bed of coals. The bass were finished first, fried in butter and peanut oil with a little sea salt and freshly ground black pepper. A few handfuls of grapes, too. I've had one whiskey and plan to have several more, and that cigar I mentioned, as I sit on the ground next to the fire.

Looking around and above me at all of this, feeling the air cool, recalling all I've experienced in one short, but eternal day I revel in the terror that is the recognition of the absolute aloneness of living this eternal existence. Concentrated days of beauty, a little truth, but not too much, that's what autumn is for me.

And while in this country the vision of the buttes that were so much apart, no all, of his landscape back home came to mind.

~ ~ ~

There are three of them standing alone out here looking like volcanoes that pushed up through the ground of the short grass prairie when no one was looking. Up this way by the Alberta border a hot wind shoves the browning grasses back and forth all day. Distant yellow fields of canola and fading emerald lakes of wheat ripple far south to Shelby and off west to peaks of the Rocky Mountain Front, snowfields blending with the miles of hazy, simmering air. A small pond below camp sparkles clear blue and sunlight flickers from its wave-broken surface, the water spring-fed and cool. Small rainbow trout leap from the surface chasing midges. Dragonflies cruise just above the water hunting down the same insects. In country that seems desolate, barren from a distance, life is everywhere. Yellow-and-white butterflies bounce around. So do grey-and-orange ones. Red-tailed hawks, Long-billed curlews, pelicans, mallards, and nighthawks dip and glide on hot patches of air or curl upwards riding the easy force of lazy whirlwinds. Sharp-tailed grouse kick up from moist draws. Spotted ground squirrels prance about like pets. Badgers growl from beneath the ground when their burrows are approached. Coyotes chatter and howl back and forth around evening. Later, a crescent moon hangs in the sky along with a rising Jupiter and some bold stars not afraid of the moon's brilliance. This land is not dead at all. It is alive in many ways.

The three buttes tower above the prairie, lower flanks covered with Blue Grama, Buffalo Grass and sage. Also, tall stems of Sweetgrass stand in isolated spots. Above this is dark grey almost black igneous rock, consisting of mostly feldspar, rock that rises steeply in ragged chunks and loose sheets for hundreds of feet, formed more than fifty million years ago, the surrounding, softer stone cut away by ice during the Bull Lake Ice Age. The buttes are like miniature island mountain ranges far out in nowhere.

Still the land is alive with a hum that sails beyond electric. The place is sacred to the Blackfeet and they fear for its vast spirit. In a way I know why. Why they feel so strongly about this place. Years ago I saw stick-like figures dancing on the northern horizon at sundown and later that night large trout leaped above the pond taking my fly before it ever hit the water. Wild, unexplainable doings. There is serious power here, not the false juice that comes from owning fancy cars, gaudy jewelry or a big house. The real thing, like all of the bodies buried in the hard ground around here.

Perhaps not for much longer. Rapacious mining interests from both Canada and this country want to level the hills and reduce the pulverized rock with a solution containing cyanide. The greedy bastards are after the gold that lies here in microscopic flakes. The mining industry doesn't give a damn about the heart of this country and what it means to the Blackfeet, people who have lived and worshipped here for centuries. Some of us who aren't tribal members love this place, too. Gold, money, power, conquest. The same perverted steps to the same old, sick dance. Level the Little Rockies. Plan to do the same along the headwaters of the Blackfoot. Destroy this country we're looking at. What's the difference? There's plenty more mountains just over the horizon. Who'd miss these three rising out where nobody really lives? Dead country to the mindless thieves. Except for the gold. That's all the fools can see. The Blackfeet believe, actually they know, that if these hills are cut down the spirits that live here will vanish. They'll fly far away. Imagine going to church, dropping on your knees and praying to a god that no longer exists for you. No all-powerful being to hear your pleas for mercy and forgiveness. Empty doesn't quite get it. No redemption this time around, kid. Try again in the next life, if you make it that far. Maybe the miners will be stopped. For now, there's always hope, but don't bet on it. The industry has lots of money and owns lots of people in all the wrong places. They'll probably get what they think they want.

My lady friend (way back behind us in the narrative she was one of the good ones if you've a mind for such trifling details) sits on the ground and looks at the middle butte, watching it change in shape and dimension beneath the moving light of the sun, the grass and rock shining with brightness. Both of us look along the low rises flowing south from the butte. A thin line of blue light, pure blue, shimmers just above the land and begins to explode into bursts of charged clouds of this unreal color. We look at each other. Are we seeing the same thing? Of course. Crazy being crazy we always see the same things even if nobody else does. What's the damn difference. You must believe everything you see before the dream spins real. We turn back to the view from here. Bolts of the light shoot back and forth among these grassy knolls and to our left a darker more intense blue sizzles up the north slope of the butte before rolling over the crest like a swirling storm cloud blowing over mountain a peak.

These edges of landscape are alive with the blue. Light fires back and forth between the hills and this lone mountain, wave after wave for hours that seem like seconds and last forever. The light just keeps flashing and then the grass at the tops of the hills shines copper and gold. Flickering beneath is the glow that pulses with a rhythm far beyond any jazz, farther along than any human beat. Time passes in a way and the blue slowly draws back into the earth as the sun begins to set, its light shading the country in soft oranges, reds and purples. Smaller bursts and bolts shoot from the ground and then the glow is gone. For now.

What the two of us experienced, we've never seen before. A shade of blue foreign to art. Unknown to photographers. Out of the reach of musicians. Beyond words. The land resonating with two humans who cannot explain what they saw but will always recognize the light whenever they see it again.

So John Wesley called it quits for the road for now and decided to come back home. He'd seen what he came to see. The vast exteriors of the land and the focused darkness of his inner self. Much of it clearly remembered. Much of it cloudy in the haze of years drifted by. He'd found what he wanted. What he needed. His sense of belonging in a world only he knew and could imagine, could move easily within. This was his gift to himself, this free ranging trip around the land. Now he was returning to his place.

### coming home

*highway glowed*
*in moonlight*
*inside instruments*
*soft green light*
*Allman Brothers*
*Hot 'Lanta*

*Jim Beam*
*plenty of it*
*sat nearby*
*Camel straights*
*on the dash*
*going fast*
*road traveled before*
*earlier*
*poured a pitcher*
*on game playing*
*woman who*
*liked morons*
*tall pines cast shadows*
*on small lakes*
*silver reflections*
*valley surrounded*
*by mountains*
*the river flows*
*in cold night*
*cigarettes burn down*
*whiskey is stale*
*keep going faster*
*heading north*
*plenty for now*

~ ~ ~

He was a little bit burned from all of the miles, all of the experiences and all of the memories. As he rounded the last curve in the dirt road to his place the sun was setting blood red, blazing orange, soft pink. The glow colored his buttes and warmed his home in the most welcome of glows. It was good to be back where he belonged, where he was happiest, at peace. He spotted the Nash Rambler station wagon of his uncommon woman friend parked off to the side of the barn and saw her, boots up on the porch railing, sitting in one of the old rockers, tall glass in her hand, bottle of Jim Beam on the deck at her side. She waved and he could see her wide, crazy smile as he drew closer.

"How in the hell did she know that I'd be back tonight?" he wondered. "Damn women spooks me half to death sometimes, most of the time. Good thing she gives me plenty of room to move or God only knows what might happen."

He waved and smiled, too.

"Damn good to be back," he said.

trip hardened

*cracked, splattered windshield*
*distorts soft things*
*that know where to*
*slice through the edges*
*drawing weary blood*
*extending seconds*
*far beyond bearable*
*and a hot wind blows*
*drying up feelings*
*that might have grown*
*in another time*
*dust swirls*
*along a narrow road*
*going nowhere*
*over an empty*
*horizon*

~ ~ ~

John Wesley finished the poetry collection. His agent sold it with a two grand advance. Decent money for poetry in this dark literary day and age. He did a few readings, and surprisingly he was mostly sober for the events. He signed books here and there all the way up to Mac's Fireweed Books in Whitehorse, Yukon and Buddy's Bookshoppe in Rocky Mountain House, Alberta. They liked him up there because he loved

Canada and its people and let his feelings show. The book, called *Plain Crazy,* actually earned back the advance in the first year, and now two years later he receives quarterly royalty checks of a size sufficient to buy some decent steaks from Terminal Meat Locker in Butte, some fine Cuban cigars whenever he's in Calgary and a little bourbon. He and the uncommon woman are very infrequent friends and lovers. On the rare occasion when they see each other at Gill's place, they sit on the front porch and watch the hours drift by, the sun set way over beyond the Rocky Mountain Front, and they sip whiskey as the stars and the moon come out and the coyotes bark and sing for the pure joy of all of it. He keeps her at a distance despite her attempts to move closer. "Move in for the kill," he thinks. "But I'll deal with that, maybe sooner rather than later." Life is good for John Wesley now. Not perfect, but good. He's learned to accept what life is these days and doesn't get angry or disappointed too often. Maybe his new love will stick and not have to disappear suddenly and mysteriously like all the others. That's confusion he hates and has no desire to experience again.

"I guess I'll drink to that, he thinks and takes a long pull from the bottle of Beam.

He looks off to the cactus garden that has now grown to the size of a modest backyard swimming pool. Sunlight flickers off a polished granite marker he had made for the spot and for his life that is inscribed ...

*The world isn't what it seems and the moment you think you've got it figured out, you're wrong*

John Wesley Gill pulls his Smith & Wesson .357 revolver out from under his chair, quickly lifts it shoulder high, pulls the trigger and shoots his latest lady friend in the head.

## Montana kid a little bit gone

*how old do you have to be*
*before you realize*
*you can't be any younger*
*you are who you are*
*and for some killing*
*comes naturally, too easy*
*before brief sanity returns*
*riding the waves*
*soaring over the plains*
*drifting down mountain canyons*
*unfamiliar but recognizable*
*laughing with mad glee*
*truly wailing this time*
*like the little*
*lonely, hurt, confused*
*kid he'll always be ...*
*After such knowledge, what forgiveness?*

Thank you for reading.
Please review this book. Reviews help others find Absolutely Amazing eBooks and inspire us to keep providing these marvelous tales.

If you would like to be put on our email list to receive updates on new releases, contests, and promotions, please go to AbsolutelyAmazingEbooks.com and sign up.

# ABOUT THE AUTHOR

John Holt is the author of two dozen published books including *Blown Away Under the Big Sky*, *The Lost Patrol*, *Yellowstone Drift - Floating the Past in Real Time*, *Arctic Aurora – Canada's Yukon and Northwest Territories*, *Coyote Nowhere - In Search of America's Last Frontier*. His work has appeared in such publications as Men's Journal, Fly Fisherman, High Country News, Crossroads, E - The Environmental Magazine, and Outside Bozeman. He and his wife, photographer Ginny Holt, live in Livingston, Montana.

# ABSOLUTELY AMAZING eBOOKS

AbsolutelyAmazingEbooks.com

or AA-eBooks.com

www.ingramcontent.com/pod-product-compliance
Lightning Source LLC
Chambersburg PA
CBHW050403030726
47503CB00006B/1991